"Liam Hu...
Bear Ridg...
ownership...

Gracie gasped.

The man beside her gasped.

She glanced down at her baby son on her lap, gnawing at his pacifier, unaware what was going on around him.

Her six-month-old had inherited a ranch? What on earth?

The lawyer peered at them over the top rim of his eyeglasses. He cleared his throat and sat back a bit.

The man beside her, who she now understood must be West Calhoun, suddenly stood up. He stared at her, then at his seventeen-pound co-owner. Now it wasn't so much tension radiating but shock. He sat back down. Ramrod straight. His gaze was now focused on the lawyer.

"Heartland Hollows Ranch," the attorney continued, "a successful working cattle operation, is valued at 8.2 million dollars."

Gracie's mouth dropped open. Million? Eight point two of them?

She couldn't digest that, so she slightly shook her head to clear it and move on to the burning issue. "I don't understand," she said, shifting Liam on her lap. She glanced at West, then turned her attention fully to the attorney. "I have no connection to that ranch. Heartland Hollows? I've never even heard of it. And I don't know anyone named Bo Bixby. There must be a mistake."

Dear Reader,

Single mom Gracie Dawson's six-month-old son has just inherited half of a very prosperous ranch. And Gracie can't figure out *why*. She and her baby boy have seemingly no connection to the Heartland Hollows cattle ranch in Bear Ridge, Wyoming. So why would the late owner have left any part of the place to a *baby*?

That's what the ranch's foreman, West Calhoun, who's inherited the *other* half, wants to know. The busy widowed father of a twelve-year-old girl, West is more than a little suspicious of Gracie. But as Christmas approaches, West and Gracie work together to figure out the connection that brought them all together...maybe as a family forever.

I hope you enjoy Gracie and West's romance. I love to hear from readers, so feel free to write me with any comments or questions (you can find contact info at my website, melissasenate.com).

Happy Holidays!

Melissa Senate

THE BABY'S CHRISTMAS RANCH

MELISSA SENATE

Harlequin

SPECIAL EDITION

If you purchased this book without a cover you should be aware that this book is stolen property. It was reported as "unsold and destroyed" to the publisher, and neither the author nor the publisher has received any payment for this "stripped book."

Harlequin® SPECIAL EDITION™

ISBN-13: 978-1-335-18013-1

The Baby's Christmas Ranch

Copyright © 2025 by Melissa Senate

All rights reserved. No part of this book may be used or reproduced in any manner whatsoever without written permission.

Without limiting the author's and publisher's exclusive rights, any unauthorized use of this publication to train generative artificial intelligence (AI) technologies is expressly prohibited.

This is a work of fiction. Names, characters, places and incidents are either the product of the author's imagination or are used fictitiously. Any resemblance to actual persons, living or dead, businesses, companies, events or locales is entirely coincidental.

For questions and comments about the quality of this book, please contact us at CustomerService@Harlequin.com.

TM and ® are trademarks of Harlequin Enterprises ULC.

Harlequin Enterprises ULC
22 Adelaide St. West, 41st Floor
Toronto, Ontario M5H 4E3, Canada
www.Harlequin.com

Printed in Lithuania

Melissa Senate has written many novels for Harlequin and other publishers, including her debut, *See Jane Date*, which was made into a TV movie. She also wrote seven books for Harlequin Special Edition under the pen name Meg Maxwell. Her novels have been published in over twenty-five countries. Melissa lives on the coast of Maine with her son; their rescue shepherd mix, Flash; and a lap cat named Cleo. For more information, please visit her website, melissasenate.com.

Books by Melissa Senate

Harlequin Special Edition

Dawson Family Ranch

Wyoming Matchmaker
His Baby No Matter What
Heir to the Ranch
Santa's Twin Surprise
The Cowboy's Mistaken Identity
Seven Birthday Wishes
Snowbound with a Baby
Triplets Under the Tree
The Rancher Hits the Road
The Cowboy's Christmas Redemption
The Rancher's Surprise Deal
The Baby's Christmas Ranch

Furever Yours

A New Leash on Love
Home is Where the Hound Is

Visit the Author Profile page
at Harlequin.com for more titles.

Dedicated in loving memory
of my mother and grandmother.

Chapter One

With her baby son on her lap, Gracie Dawson sat in a lawyer's office with no idea why she was there. Last week, a certified letter had requested she—*and her six-month-old*—arrive at 10:00 a.m. today for the reading of a will. From the moment she'd signed for that letter she'd tried to figure out who might have included her in their will. She hadn't lost anyone recently, not since her grandfather died six years ago.

Her mom and grandmother had been so curious that they'd insisted on scouring the obituaries in the *Bear Ridge Free Weekly* and the *Brewer County Gazette*. They'd called out names of the departed to see if Gracie had known them. A little morbid, but nope. None of the names was even familiar.

Her grandmother, Dorothea, was sure Gracie had done a nice thing for someone, maybe even ten, twenty years ago and had forgotten all about it—whereas the recipient of her kindness had not and had left her a small token of appreciation. *You're a nice person!* her gram had added.

They'd all liked that idea. Gracie did tend to go out of her way to lend a hand. But then her mom, Linda

Dawson, pointed out that Gracie would at least recognize a name among the departed.

And, her father, Larry Dawson, had added, *Why would Gracie need to bring a baby to the reading? It must be a* recent *thing.*

Probably, Gracie had thought. Then her mom had said what they'd all been thinking but hadn't wanted to bring up since the subject tended to leave them *all* feeling unsettled.

The father of Gracie's baby.

A cowboy named Harry Ahern. A couple years older than Gracie at twenty-nine, he'd disappeared on her the day she'd told him she was pregnant. And just three months after Liam was born six months ago, she'd been shaken to learn that Harry had died in a daredevil jump on a motorcycle. But six months wasn't all that recent.

Except when probate comes into play, her dad had said. *Sometimes that whole rigmarole takes a while. Years, even.*

They'd all nodded since that had sounded plausible.

Still, Gracie highly doubted the will reading was connected to the cowboy who'd said he lived hand to mouth and had no family. What could there possibly be in probate? Harry had told her he was a "rolling stone," that he hadn't even owned a car let alone a home, that he'd always taken ranch jobs that offered room and board, and spent his paycheck a little too fast.

No, she couldn't imagine Harry Ahern had left her—or their son—a thing considering he'd walked out of her life when she'd been two months pregnant.

She'd had a week to wonder and wait, and now she was here, so curious. Not two minutes ago, an admin had led her into the office, gestured at one of two guest chairs facing the large cherrywood desk, and let her know the attorney would be in shortly.

She was lucky to have today off. Gracie worked as a ranch hand at the Dawson Family Guest Ranch, owned by her cousins, who'd been kind enough to hire her. They hadn't actually had any openings, but when she'd been fired from her last job for being "unable to fulfill her duties as a hand" when she got to be seven months along, her cousin Daisy had assured her that after her maternity leave, she would work at the guest ranch as often and little as she wanted as a stringer. That had meant helping out in any capacity they needed, whether as a ranch hand, in the cafeteria or day care center, where she could bring her baby son. Gracie had enjoyed the variety the past few months. Her mom and gram were all too happy to watch their little grandson when she wasn't assigned to the day care.

Gracie pulled out her phone to check the time. It was still a few minutes until ten, but she was anxious to find out what this was about.

As she heard someone come in, she turned. A man she didn't know but recognized from around town was being led in by the admin. Not the attorney if his jeans, flannel shirt and cowboy boots were anything to go by. He held on to a brown cowboy hat, probably a Stetson given the quality. Early thirties, she'd say. Tall, over six feet. Lanky but with muscles. Tousled dark hair. Blue eyes. She'd noticed him over the years in Bear Ridge because he was very good-looking. And because he was always with a little girl who looked just like him. Though, now that Gracie thought about it, the last time she'd seen him, sitting outside the coffee shop a few months ago, that little girl had grown up. Tweenage.

He must be named in the will too. As he approached the guest chair, he stopped for a second and stared at her, his eyes narrowing as though he was trying to figure something out, then he sat down. A tension radiated off him. He gave baby Liam a glance, but he didn't even smile the way people did at the sight of a baby inches from them. He turned away from where she sat beside him, his gaze out the window. There was nothing but an evergreen to look at, so he was clearly avoiding any potential small talk. Okay, then.

Suddenly the man turned toward her and said, "How did you know Bi—"

He was interrupted by the lawyer's arrival, his question forgotten as they both sat up straight in anticipation. In his fifties, with black round glasses, the attorney introduced himself as Garland Jones, moved behind the desk and sat, two manila envelopes in front of him along with a file folder. He asked for their IDs, which made Gracie frown. ID?

With an arm carefully around Liam, she reached into her tote bag hanging from the push bar of the stroller beside her chair. She leaned forward to hand the attorney her driver's license, as did the man. Garland Jones studied the licenses, handed them back, and Gracie waited on the ole pins and needles. *What was this all about?*

"Without further ado," the attorney said, sliding out documents from the envelopes. "First, per the last will and testament of Bo Bixby...

"West Calhoun, age thirty-four, of Bear Ridge, Wyoming, foreman of the Heartland Hollows Ranch, shall inherit half ownership of the estate, including but not limited to the land, house, animals, cabins, outbuildings and equipment."

The man beside her moved his hand to his chest. She glanced at his face, but his expression was unreadable. He glanced at her—the eyes narrowing even more. *He's waiting to see why I'm here*, she realized. *Just like I am.*

"Second," the attorney continued, "Liam Hurley Dawson, age six months, of Bear Ridge, Wyoming, shall inherit equal half ownership of the Heartland Hollows Ranch."

Gracie gasped.

The man beside her gasped.

She glanced down at her baby son on her lap, gnawing at his pacifier, unaware what was going on around him.

Her *six-month-old* inherited a ranch? *What on earth?*

The lawyer peered at them over the top rim of his eyeglasses. He cleared his throat and sat back a bit.

The man beside her, who she now understood must be West Calhoun, suddenly stood up. He stared at her then at his seventeen-pound co-owner. Now it wasn't so much tension radiating but shock. He sat back down. Ramrod-straight. His gaze was now focused on the lawyer.

"Heartland Hollows Ranch," the attorney continued, "a successful working cattle operation, is valued at 8.2 million dollars."

Gracie's mouth dropped open. *Million*—8.2 of them?

She couldn't digest that, so slightly shook her head to clear it and move on to the burning issue. "I don't understand," she said, shifting Liam on her lap. She glanced at West, then turned her attention fully to the attorney. "I have no connection to that ranch. Heartland Hollows? I've never even heard of it. And I don't know *anyone* named Bo Bixby. There must be a mistake." Obviously.

She could feel West Calhoun's eyes on her. She glanced at him, and now confusion seemed to be mixed in with the shock.

"No mistake," the attorney said. "Bo, who was an old friend of mine, by the way, was quite clear in his wishes." He patted the document. "He left a letter for me to read to the both of you after the bequeathment was read."

Gracie leaned forward. A letter? Just what was she about to learn?

The foreman—West Calhoun—exhaled hard. No doubt he had the same question.

First things first, West thought, shifting his six-foot-two-inch frame in the hard leather chair.

No matter how deeply moved he was to discover that Bo had left him any part of the ranch or how... surprised that a *baby* had inherited equal ownership with him, his heart felt too heavy to keep him upright.

Bo Bixby was gone. And West was grieving the loss hard. Even his twelve-year-old daughter—who'd morphed from upbeat sidekick to instant tweenhood with constant earbuds and an exasperated *Dad!* to most things he said—had been a little more pleasant to him the past week. A few days ago, Alexa had kept peering at him in the barn as they'd done some chores together, Taylor Swift blaring from her earbuds to the point that he could hear the lyrics, and she'd taken out an earbud and said, *Are you okay, Daddy?* in a small, tentative voice. He'd kneeled down beside her on the straw-covered stall, something he could still do like she was a little kid since he was almost a foot taller, and assured her he was okay, that he was just sad about Bo. She'd nodded and said she was too. Alexa had lived on the ranch since she was two years old, the only home she could remember. She'd also actually let him hug her, which had done good things for his heart, but she'd wriggled away after a few seconds and popped the earbud back in.

He'd seen for himself in the mirror yesterday morning that he still had a sadness in his eyes to go along with the lump lodged in his throat, uncharacteristic tears threatening at just the sight of little things that reminded him of his boss. Let alone the entire ranch itself, where West had spent the last ten years. In that time, he himself had morphed from a lost, grieving widowed cowboy with a two-year-old daughter to seasoned foreman who tried his hardest every day to balance his home and work life.

Put that girl of yours first, Bo had said more than a few times over the years when West had had to take time off from the ranch due to Alexa's strep throat or parent-teacher conferences. His parents were long gone, and though Alexa's maternal grandparents were a loving force in her life, they lived over an hour away in the same town as their younger daughter, a divorced mom of ten-year-old triplets. West had always had his hands full.

Again, West's heart clenched deep in his chest. Bo, his mentor, his dear friend—gone. A father figure when West's own dad had died when he was very young.

Not that Bo had been an easy man. The workaholic rancher had been taciturn, reserved, and hard to get to know—to the point that the first five years West had worked for Heartland Hollows as a cowboy, the two had said maybe three words to each other. West would be guiding the herd out on the range and suddenly he'd notice Bo on horseback, surveying, watching. The sight of the solitary, unsmiling ranch owner watching him and the other cowboys had always sent a chill up West's spine. He could be fired any minute and, with a child to raise, he couldn't lose his job. But when Bo's long-time foreman retired five years ago, Bo had called West into the office. He'd been recommended for the job and Bo had added that he'd been watching West for years, taking note of his skill, his professionalism, his integrity. West would never forget the way he'd felt in that office.

They'd gotten somewhat close the past five years, not that Bo ever discussed anything personal. Except the previous six months—about the cancer that was taking him both slowly and fast. Bo had no family, and if there had been a woman in his life, she certainly hadn't made an appearance in those difficult months. West had been there, including at Bo's bedside toward the terrible end, and when this man who'd meant so much to him had taken his last breath.

Chubby-cheeked Liam Hurley Dawson, casually sucking on a pacifier as though he hadn't just inherited half of a very prosperous Wyoming ranch, and the woman on whose lap he sat, certainly hadn't been there. What the hell was the connection between her and Bo? Nothing got past West at the Heartland Hollows Ranch. If she'd come around to see Bo, West would have known.

Wait.

The baby was six months old, which meant if she'd set her sights on a wealthy, older rancher, it would have been last year. For all West knew, she'd been Bo's secret girlfriend—before he'd gotten sick. She was very attractive with her long honey-blond hair and big green eyes. Minimal makeup, if any. A gold ID-style bracelet on one wrist with initials on it that West couldn't read from where he sat. She wore a camel-colored sweater, dark jeans and cowboy boots. Understated. Save the sweater, she was dressed just like he was. Certainly not the outfit or look of a gold-digger.

Still, who knew? Maybe Bo had met her in town, fallen fast and hard, and had set her up with a house or condo where they'd had their dalliances. Maybe Bo had confided in her that he'd been diagnosed with pancreatic cancer and she hadn't wanted to deal with that. It was possible she'd told Bo she was pregnant with his baby and figured he'd leave a good inheritance to his only child. So she'd ghosted him—and waited.

And today was payday.

It wasn't like West to think the worst of someone, but...

He'd gauge her age at twenty-eight tops. Bo had been sixty-two. That was some age difference.

Except... She'd just said a minute ago that she didn't know anyone named Bo Bixby. And to admit that when her kid inherited half the Heartland Hollows? Coming straight out with having zero connection to Bo or Heartland Hollows wouldn't do her any favors if he contested the will, not that he would. If Bo had had named this baby in the will, he'd done so for a reason.

He glanced at the blonde again, assessing her. Studying her. It was almost as if she'd been expecting to hear that *yes*, the whole thing was a mistake, and she'd have a funny story to share with her family and friends later. *Remember that time Liam "inherited" a half-a-zillion-dollar ranch when he was six months old? Hahahaha!*

Nothing about this made sense.

Maybe the letter Bo had written would explain. Surely, it *would*.

The lawyer cleared his throat again and removed a

white sheet of paper from a folder. West could see it was handwritten—Bo's easily recognizable scrawl. "If you're both ready," he said, peering at them.

The woman nodded. West nodded. Even the baby seemed to be nodding.

"'To Gracie Dawson, mother of Liam Dawson, and to West Calhoun...'" Garland Jones began.

West sucked in a breath and leaned forward.

"'I, Bo Bixby, in sound mind, leave half the Heartland Hollows Ranch to my trusted foreman and dear friend West Calhoun. I leave the other half to Liam Dawson, a baby boy born in Bear Ridge Hospital on June second of this year. Until Liam Dawson reaches age twenty-one, his inheritance is to be managed by his mother, Gracie Dawson. Yours, Bo Bixby.'"

He slid the letter back into the file folder, then looked at up at them, folding his hand on the desk.

Gracie's neck jutted forward. "Is that *it*?" she asked, looking very confused.

"Yes, that's the extent of the letter," the lawyer said.

She shook her head. "But, there *must* be more information. Particularly why a man I've never met would leave half his ranch to a baby *he's* never met."

Yes, I'd *like to know that, too*, West thought.

"I'm afraid I don't have additional information," the attorney said.

West wasn't surprised. If West didn't know anything about Gracie Dawson's connection to Bo, the lawyer sure wouldn't, old friend or not. In the ten years West had known Bo and lived on the same property as him, he'd certainly never seen Garland Jones, esquire, at the ranch. The two might go way back and Bo might have trusted the man, but they weren't buddies.

West had a feeling that Gracie Dawson knew more than she realized. He felt himself brightening at the thought. Yes, that had to be it. She held the key to the connection, and West wanted to know what it was.

"Excuse me, Mr. Jones," Gracie suddenly said. "Does the name Harry Ahern mean anything to you?" She sounded tentative, as if she was trying out the name on her lips.

The lawyer thought for a moment. "No. Doesn't ring a bell at all."

"What about you?" she asked West.

"Harry Ahern?" West shook his head. He didn't know anyone by that name.

He was about to ask Gracie why she'd brought him up, but the attorney straightened the folders on his desk, then started explaining that he'd been named executor of the will, had copies for each of them, including the letter, and all pertinent documents requiring signature. He also requested their email addresses so that certain documents could be signed electronically and set two brief forms on his desk, facing them.

West watched Gracie smooth the baby's blond hair and settle him into the stroller beside her chair, the clicks of the harness jolting him in the silence of the office. She then leaned toward the desk and filled out the form, West doing the same.

There was a bit more legal jargon, and then the attorney stood and thanked them for coming in and wished them a "prosperous partnership."

West froze. This was real. His partner was a baby.

A tiny toothless human—with seemingly no connection anyone in this room knew of to Bo Bixby.

West let out a sigh, aware suddenly that Gracie's eyes had darted his way.

She reached in the stroller basket for what looked like a mini sleeping bag with arms. She got the baby bundled into it, stood, nodded at the attorney and extended her hand to him for a shake, then turned to leave the office.

Well, wait a minute. They had to talk. Figure this all out.

West followed her into the reception area, where the admin was sitting behind a desk, typing at a keyboard. He and Gracie Dawson stopped at the coatrack. He slipped into his heavy barn jacket and watched Gracie put on a knee-length, down silver-gray coat. She wrapped a fuzzy multicolored scarf around her neck, then reached for the matching wool hat and settled that on her head. Wool gloves were next.

"I..." he began, but the situation, this woman—this *baby* partner—had him all upside down. He couldn't even get words out.

Gracie glanced up at him, waiting, curiosity in her green eyes. That was positive. At least they were both completely at a loss together.

The admin stood and headed down a short hallway, he assumed to give them privacy.

"You..." she began, but then also stopped talking.

He waited a beat, but Gracie didn't finish what she'd been about to say—or reach for the door. She seemed unsure of herself, nervous, even. He had a strange pang of sympathy for her. If she was telling the truth about not knowing Bo, then this had to be as shocking for her as it was for him.

He cleared his throat like the lawyer. This couldn't be more awkward. "If you have a little time," he said, settling his Stetson on his head. "I could show you the ranch—Heartland Hollows—and we could talk. Try to unravel your baby's connection to Bo."

It's there, somewhere, he knew.

The relief on her face had him glad he'd offered. There was something genuine about her, but maybe he was just needing that to be true. Between running the ranch and trying to regain his connection with his daughter, he didn't want to add worrying about Gracie Dawson's motives or intentions for her child's half of the ranch to the load on his shoulders, which were already weighed down with the loss of Bo.

"You can follow me in your car," he said. "The ranch is ten minutes from here."

She nodded. "I'll do that."

This was good. He'd have ten minutes to himself, to think, to process. To work out how he felt about all this, though he was sure he'd need a lot more time than ten minutes.

But once they were at the house and talking, he could get a better sense of her.

The baby might be his new co-owner, but Gracie Dawson would be his partner for the next *twenty and a half years*.

Chapter Two

Gracie held her breath when West's silver pickup truck, which she was following down a winding rural road, slowed as they approached a sign for the Heartland Hollows Ranch. Engraved on metal, large and ornate, it featured the ranch's name, that it had been established in 1899, and a logo—a cowboy silhouetted on a horse, a group of cattle beside them. That was something—1899. Had it been passed down from generation to generation of Bixbys?

She wished she could pull over and Google that—find out what she could in an online search about Bo Bixby and the ranch. Maybe something would pop up that would make the revelations of this morning make sense.

But she could hardly do that right now. Everything would come clear, hopefully in the talk the foreman had suggested, which she was grateful for. She was hardly thinking straight, so she appreciated that they were going to sit down together and figure this out.

She followed West up the long gravel-packed drive, flanked by evergreens with a slight dusting of the snow they'd gotten a few days ago. An open, wide gate, also ornate metal, the same sign atop it, greeted her. Just beyond was an elegant white farmhouse with a wrap-around porch and a pretty red barn with a weathervane atop it. A big green wreath had been hung on the side of the barn, a testament to Christmas coming, though it was just the first week of December.

West pulled up into a circular paved drive in front of the house and she parked behind him. She took in a deep breath. Was any of this real? She wouldn't be surprised if she awoke suddenly to Liam's cry and realized this had all been just a dream.

She gave her wrist a pinch to check. *Ow.* She was wide awake.

Okay, let's go see what's what. As she stepped out to untether Liam's car seat, she glanced up ahead. Land stretched as far as she could see, mountains in the distance. About a quarter mile toward the mountains were two big gray barns, a small group of hands and cowboys milling about, unloading a hay delivery. There were large herds of cattle in the far pastures enjoying the not-cold day. Forty-three degrees on a December morning in Wyoming was a welcome surprise.

There was a rustic elegance to the place. Heartland Hollows was a working cattle ranch yet there seemed a separation between the main house with its almost decorative-looking red barn just across the path. The barn was likely for storage or maybe even held the ranch office. The main action of Heartland Hollows seemed to happen where the gray barns and pastures and employees were.

She noted West had gotten out of his truck and was

walking toward her. A half hour ago, she'd never met the man. Suddenly he was the only familiar thing about this place. *That* was strange. But so was everything connected to the reading of the will.

She carried the car seat, Liam napping at the moment, over to the cargo area to get out the stroller. She should have gotten the stroller first, then the seat, but to say she was distracted was an understatement.

"I'll get the stroller base," West said, stepping to the tailgate. He got it open and lugged out the collapsed base, then snapped it open in two seconds. If she hadn't known he had a child from seeing them around Bear Ridge over the years, his stroller skills would have clued her in.

She settled the car seat into the base, heard its sturdy clicks. "Thanks." She turned, looking toward the house. "This place is so beautiful."

"It is. The entire ranch, from the house and cabins to the outbuildings and fields, were Bo's life. His pride and joy. The slightest paint chip was fixed immediately. He always had the wreath up every December first, so I continued the tradition." He gestured up at the red barn.

She looked over at it and smiled, talk of the upcoming holiday, the sight of the festive wreath, making her feel a bit more comfortable.

"I live in the foreman's cabin and have for the past five years," he said, pointing up ahead where the gray barns were. "The cabin is nestled into the woods about a quarter mile to the left of the barns down a stone pathway. My daughter thinks it's like a fairy-tale cottage. It's definitely more a cozy, nice home than typical ranch cabin, so she's not wrong."

That got another smile out of her. "How old is your daughter?" she asked—suddenly wondering about the girl's mother. All these years she'd noticed him and his daughter in town, there had never been a woman. Or wait, maybe she had seen a woman many years ago, when the girl was very young. She couldn't remember.

"Twelve," he said. "Newly a tween. I don't exist. Well, really I shouldn't say that. Two days ago, Alexa caught me looking sad about Bo and not only asked how I was doing, but gave me a hug."

She tilted her head. "Well, that says a lot of wonderful things about your relationship. I remember being a tween. Not an easy time for the kid or the parents."

He nodded. "Tell me about it. And I'm the *sole* parent. Her mother died ten years ago. Car accident," he added, looking away toward the mountains for a moment.

Her heart went out to him. "I'm sorry. Can't be easy raising a girl on your own."

"It's not. What's that saying about your heart walking around outside your body—forever?"

Huh. This man kept catching her off guard, saying things she didn't expect. She looked at her sleeping child. "Now *that*, I know something about."

West looked at Liam in the stroller. "He seems like a good baby. Barely made a peep at the reading."

She nodded with a smile. "I got lucky with this little guy. No sign of his first tooth yet, though. Any day now, I'm sure he'll be cranky on a regular basis."

He laughed, and she found herself relaxing again, the camaraderie between them nice. "Let's head in. I'll show you around and make us coffee."

She nodded and they walked toward the house. It was so lovely and majestic, yet not overwhelming. As they approached the porch steps, West deftly picked up the entire stroller and carried it up. "Thanks," she said. "Though I've added a few muscles from lugging this up the steps at my house. And I was plenty strong before Liam came along. I've been a ranch hand since I was eighteen. Lots of mucking out stalls, chasing after runaway goats at my last place."

He was staring at her with that same confusion he'd had in the lawyer's office. She wondered what he was thinking.

But all thought poofed from her head when he opened the door. The interior was a perfect mix of modern and rustic with wood beams on the ceilings, arched doorways, a huge stone fireplace, antique furniture and expensive Western-style rugs. A beautiful staircase with an ornate wood banister led to a second story. She felt like she was in a pricey vacation home.

"Wow," she said. "This house."

"I know," he said, glancing around himself. "I'd worked for Heartland Hollows for years before I ever got invited inside. Not what I was expecting, though I didn't know what I'd expected from Bo. Maybe more of a sparse bachelor pad."

Bachelor pad. So this Bo Bixby hadn't been married? Maybe divorced or widowed. Was there a woman's touch in the furnishings? As Gracie looked around, she really couldn't tell, but she'd say no.

West set down the stroller, and she managed to get Liam out of his winter bunting without waking him up. As she held Liam, West took the bunting and put it in a basket by the door. He helped her out of her coat, always awkward while holding a baby, and hung up their gear on a wrought-iron coatrack.

Gallant. That was always nice.

He showed her the rooms on the first level, the large kitchen that was modern yet still warm and inviting. An office/den with a stately desk and leather chair, a map of Wyoming and a few black-and-white blown-up shots of the ranch on the deep gray walls. A half bathroom, which was bigger than either of the full baths in her family home was. And the living room, with its wall of windows that included sliding-glass doors to the deck and that gorgeous huge stone fireplace and comfortable furnishings.

Up the elegant staircase, she could see down a wide hall with open doors. West led her to the rooms. The primary suite, decidedly masculine with its dark brown leather headboard and wood touches, was large with its own very-updated bathroom. West showed her another guest bathroom in the hall, and the three additional bedrooms, all furnished with antiques and neutral décor.

"What a beautiful home," she said. The word *home* echoed in her ears. She still couldn't process what the lawyer had read in his office—about six-month-old

Liam and West Calhoun *together* inheriting the estate, including this house and everything in it.

The series of small oil paintings of buffalo on the hallway wall was half Liam's? The runner? The toothpaste in the bathroom? The entire contents of this glorious house? How did this make sense?

When Gracie had woken up that morning, she'd been the same struggling single mother she'd been the past many months, trying to sock away enough money for the required down payment to qualify for a first-time home buyer's plan on a small house for herself and Liam. She'd worked hard. She was frugal. And she didn't want to rely on her always-generous parents, who'd give her their last dollar. She'd had to move back in with the Dawsons after discovering she was pregnant since the cabin she'd shared with another female hand would have been out of the question with a baby. But it was important to Gracie to make a home for herself and her son. She'd been worried, though. About finances and what the future held.

Now, this entire ranch was Liam's—even half? There had to be a catch. Or an explanation. She certainly didn't feel at home and didn't expect to even after everything became clear. If it ever did.

She and West Calhoun would have that talk he'd mentioned. The truth was somewhere and they'd find it.

"Ready for that coffee?" he asked, West's blue eyes on her.

He clearly wanted the truth too. He had to be wondering at the connection between Bo Bixby and her son since she'd said she hadn't known Bo, had never heard of the ranch.

She let out a breath. "Definitely."

He smiled and led the way.

She followed him down the stairs, where he stopped to pick up Liam's car seat from the entryway, and into the bright kitchen. He set the car seat on the big round table by a beautiful bay window that faced the red barn and pastures. Gracie settled her still-napping son into the seat and latched the harness, hoping the clicks wouldn't wake him up. They didn't.

"Good napper," West said, his gaze soft on the baby for a moment. He turned to Gracie. "Alexa, on the other hand—I definitely don't want to remember her two-minute naps and hour-long screech fests."

Gracie smiled. "That bad?"

"Napping was never her thing. *Now*, she could sleep through a herd of bulls on the roof." He moved to the cabinets and opened one near the sink. "Any preference on coffee? Bo had a few unopened bags of his favorites—" He stopped talking suddenly and just stood there, his back to her, not moving a muscle. He seemed…frozen.

Ah. Bo's coffee. Bo's kitchen. Bo's house. Bo Bixby—the man who'd left West half the place. They'd had to have been close. West had lost someone special to him.

"Reminders, am I right?" she asked gently, looking from him to the coffee on the shelves.

He turned with a bag of coffee in his hand and nodded. "Bo wasn't much of a socializer, but when he got diagnosed, he'd often asked if I'd stop by for coffee on my way back from dropping Alexa at the school bus stop, and it became a daily thing. We'd talk about the ranch, the staff, the weather. Toward the end, he'd said several times that he'd made a few mistakes and was trying to make some peace with that. I let him know I was here to listen if he ever wanted to get anything off his chest, but he never did. The last week, he didn't talk much at all, just would hold my hand."

"Oh, West," she said, her hand to her heart. She hadn't experienced that kind of loss of someone close to her—where you knew they were dying and were present for it until the end. Her grandfather had died peacefully in his sleep. How painful those six months must have been for West.

"I'm no stranger to losing someone I love. But I guess there was something in raising my daughter in her mother's honor that gave me a feeling of purpose. Now, I just feel...*reminded* that there are no guarantees." He seemed to wince, as though he was embarrassed by sharing that with her. "Stop being so easy to talk to," he said, a poignant smile on his handsome face.

How her heart went out to him just then. If it would be even remotely appropriate, she'd give West Calhoun a hug. Acquaintance to acquaintance. Except they were co-owners of a ranch under unusual circumstances. There was a level of unspoken complication here.

He quickly started making the coffee, then rooted around in the fridge, pulling out a carton of half-and-half. "I cleaned out the fridge and freezer entirely, but

I left some things that were unopened. And opened but still good, like the creamer. Bo would go to the fridge every morning to get it while he could still get around easily. I couldn't bear to throw it out."

"Bo left half the ranch to you, half to Liam—he had no family?" she asked.

He shook his head, carrying over two mugs of coffee, which he set down on the table, followed by a sugar bowl and the cream. "No immediate family that I know of, no relatives. For all I could tell the past ten years, Bo Bixby was alone in the world."

She sat, stirring in some cream. It might be a tiny thing but she felt a connection to Bo Bixby. The man had left her baby half his beloved ranch. What was the link between the two? If he had no family, the connection couldn't be related to Liam's father. But then what?

"He never married? No kids? No family is no family, but I guess I'm just surprised. It's not common, I suppose. Particularly among ranchers."

West nodded. "If he married and had kids, I certainly never heard of any wives or ex-wives or kids. And in the ten years I've worked for Heartland Hollows, I never saw *anyone* go into the house. He was a loner. I wonder if he even had any romantic relationships at all."

"Maybe he did before he bought this place and got hurt so badly that he swore off love?" she said, her voice questioning. "I have an uncle who did that after his divorce, but thankfully they were famous last words and he fell madly in love again."

"Could be," West said. "I sure did for a few years after my wife died."

That got her attention. A few years single? "So you remarried?"

"No. I just became open to dating the past couple of years. I rationalized it by thinking Alexa would benefit from a loving stepmother. But..."

She gave him a gentle smile. "Yeah, I know that *but* from my own experience with dating. Being open to it doesn't put the right person next to you."

She'd learned that before she'd ever met Harry Ahern and she was hardly open to dating now. She couldn't imagine when she would be.

He nodded, then stirred some sugar in his coffee and turned away slightly. She had the sense he didn't like talking about this.

"So, Heartland Hollows—it was established in 1899," she said. "Cleary not by Bixbys. Bo bought it with that name."

He nodded. "The ranch had changed hands many times over the years, four different owners. Everyone kept the Heartland Hollows since they liked that it had such a long history in town, like the sign too."

"Makes sense," she said, taking another sip of her coffee. "Did Bo grow up in Bear Ridge?" she asked. "Live here his whole life?"

West shook his head. "He bought this place ten years ago, right before I hired on. I'm pretty sure he moved from Brewer or maybe a small town where he'd had another ranch. I don't think he ever mentioned what town." Brewer was a large, bustling town about a half hour away. West grabbed his phone and typed into the tiny keyboard. "Bo Bixby. Wyoming. Let's see if anything comes up that stands out." He scrolled. "Just hits about Heartland Hollows and some cattle auction sales. Nothing I don't already know."

Gracie nodded and sat back, wracking her brain to figure out any type of connection between her and Bixby. *Could* she have done him a favor without realizing it, like her grandmother had wondered? He'd have left the ranch to *her* then. Was there a family link she didn't know about? She'd check with her parents and grandmother—maybe they knew Bo? No—now that she thought about it, his name had come up in the obituaries they'd rattled off, so they would have said something. It hadn't rung a bell, just like it hadn't with her.

West sipped his coffee. "You asked the lawyer and me if we knew a Harry Ahern. Possible connection between your son and Bo?"

"I can't imagine there is. Harry Ahern is Liam's father. He died in a motorcycle accident just a few months after Liam was born."

"Sorry," he said, shaking his head. "There's so much damned loss. You're widowed too?"

Her stomach clenched. She took a fast sip of the fragrant coffee to hide her expression. "We weren't married. We'd been dating just a month when I told him I was pregnant. God, his face at the news."

She glanced at West, who was looking at her with compassion.

Gracie sucked in a breath. "He told me he wasn't cut out to be a father and left. I thought I'd give him an hour to digest the news, but when I tried to call him, I discovered he'd blocked me." She bit her lip at the hard memory, nothing she wanted to think about. Her stomach had ached for hours when she'd made the discovery that he'd actually blocked her, the tear in her heart so jagged it never had really smoothed over.

Why had she told West all that? She winced, wishing she could take it all back.

"I have a great family," she said fast, needing to change the subject to something much more pleasant. "My parents have been an incredible support system. My grandmother too. They watch Liam when I'm at work. I'm a stringer at the Dawson Family Guest Ranch—cousins of mine own it."

"I know it well," he said, looking at her intently. "You've been through a lot, Gracie."

She nodded. He had too. She sat with that for a moment. "What I can't figure out is why or how Bo knew about Liam—including where he was born and his birthday. That information was in the letter the attorney read. How would Bo know about that? And *why*?"

"There must be something we're both missing," West said. "The name Harry Ahern definitely isn't familiar, but Bo didn't talk about his personal life, so if he knew someone by that name, I wouldn't necessarily be aware of that. Did Harry ever come back to talk about you two co-parenting?"

She shook her head. "I never saw or heard from him again after the day I told him I was pregnant." She lifted her chin, trying to ward off those old feelings that always hurt. Her child's father had just walked away. She looked over at Liam in his car seat, sleeping so peacefully. She'd never understand how Harry hadn't cared in the slightest. She drank down some more coffee, needing the comfort of the hot cup.

West seemed about say something but was interrupted by a suddenly unhappy Liam.

"Waaa! Waaa!"

So much for not being a fussy baby. Liam was now crying and waving around his arms.

Gracie was almost grateful for the interruption of their conversation. They'd gotten personal fast. Maybe because they'd been thrust into a strange new situation together. The need for an ally warred with everything telling her to be cautious around West Calhoun until she knew he was as trustworthy as he seemed. *Seemed* could hide a lot. Who knew that better than she did?

She moved over to Liam and picked him up, rubbing his back while swaying a bit. Still screeching.

"Maybe a little gas," West said.

She glanced at the man in surprise until she remembered he'd been through this himself. She gave Liam's back a few pats. No burp. She kept rocking him, hoping he'd settle down, but he didn't. "It's a little early for his lunch, but maybe he's hungry. I have his bottle and formula with me, if you don't mind?"

"Of course not," he said. "I'll hold him while you make up the bottle."

She turned and looked at West, this time the surprise sticking around. That was nice of him. *Because he's a dad himself*, she reminded herself. She was used to single cowboys on the ranches she'd worked at. The word *baby* itself made a few of them turn pale. "I appreciate that. Maybe a change of arms will help him calm down."

She handed Liam over, not that the baby went gently.

West took him expertly, though, cuddling him against his chest and the soft flannel shirt. He rubbed his back and started humming "Hush Little Baby," which made her smile for a second in the middle of being stressed. Maybe she had to accept that West Calhoun would constantly surprise her. At some point, she'd accept that he was a good guy, a nice guy, and calm down around him. He sure seemed to be.

He sang and hummed since he didn't seem to remember all the words. Gracie found herself smiling again.

Liam kept crying, though. Even harder.

She grabbed the bottle and formula from the stroller basket, then made up the bottle by the sink, giving it a good shake. "Okay, ready."

"Sorry," West said. "Usually babies love me."

She smiled, though it faded fast since her son was in distress. "I really appreciate that you tried. He's either hungry or has a bellyache. Or maybe a tooth *is* trying to poke up through sore gums." He handed over the baby, and Liam did settle down a little bit, back in familiar arms. She tried to offer him the bottle, but he kept turning his head, his sweet little face getting red. "Huh. Maybe it is a tooth coming. I have some baby gum reliever at home. I can try that. And some bicycle pumps for his legs." She stood up and got Liam back into the stroller. "I'd better get him home."

West nodded. As she poured out the contents of the bottle and rinsed it, he said, "I mentioned that my daughter and I live in the foreman's cabin. We're very happy there. So you're welcome to the house."

She gasped before she could stop herself. She hadn't gotten that far—thinking about anything in connection with the inheritance other than why a total stranger left a baby his estate. "I've lived in either tiny hand cabins on ranches I've worked for or with my parents, where I've been living since the last months of the pregnancy. An entire house—and such a nice one. This definitely doesn't feel real."

"Bo's will says it is and there's no need to delay. Why don't you plan to move in tomorrow and when you're ready to take a break, we can meet to discuss the basics of Heartland Hollows. Ownership is new to me, too, but I was Bo's right-hand man on every aspect of management, including the financials. I basically ran the place myself the past six months, so everything should continue on seamlessly. You don't have to involve yourself in the ranch at all—I'll keep you in the loops in all regards."

She took that in—and could feel herself bristling. Was this a bit of the *real* West Calhoun coming out? She had no intention of letting West run roughshod over her.

"As I've said, I'm a ranch hand by trade," she said. "Hardly a foreman with that level of management experience, but as I'm tasked with managing my son's stake in this ranch, I intend to be *fully* involved. I'm smart, a quick study, and I work hard. If you're worried about me slowing you down or any monkey wrenches, rest assured that won't be the case." She lifted her chin, keeping her eyes on his.

"I'm actually very glad to hear all of that," he said. "And I didn't mean any offense. Just giving you options. To be honest, having an equal partner who cares about this ranch as much as I do is a huge comfort, Gracie."

Huh. He'd managed to surprise her *again*. She certainly hadn't expected *that* to come out of his mouth. She tossed the bottle into the stroller basket, then extended her hand.

He smiled and they shook. She liked the feel of his hand. Strong, warm. There was just something about West that made her believe he *was* a good guy, that she could count on him, even. He'd been open about quite a lot and so had she.

Building some trust. She'd stay on alert, of course. But her gut told her he was true blue. Her trust level in strangers had been low since Harry Ahern. So, that West had passed muster with her said something.

Who knew, though? Maybe it said, *You're gullible*. Harry had seemed a great guy too. Being a rolling stone hadn't meant he was a bad person, just that he didn't collect moss. And that should given her pause. But she'd been too taken with him to let it. Story of a thousand broken hearts, hers included.

So just keep your guard up. Be smart. Be sensible. She would be.

"In terms of income," West added, "Bo took a salary, enough to be comfortable but nowhere near what he could have. I suggest we follow his lead and each draw what he did, which is closer to what would be standard for a ranch owner." He named a figure that was more than three times her current salary as a ranch hand and she had to hold back her gasp. "I'll forego my salary as foreman but continue in that role."

She was speechless for a moment—until Liam reminded her that he needed to get home. She bent down a bit to run a hand over his soft hair, then she straightened and turned to West. "Well, trust that I'll be the hardest-working ranch hand at Heartland Hollows. The more I learn, the more experience I gain, the more I can contribute."

He briefly talked a bit more about finances and projections, but then he said he was probably getting ahead of himself since she hadn't had a chance to read over the paperwork the attorney had promised to send.

Tonight, she'd do some research about Heartland Hollows, including the papers that the lawyer had given her, and she'd be ready for West at the meeting.

She might have a good feeling about West Calhoun's character, but she had to remind herself that she *didn't* know him.

She would not forget it.

Chapter Three

At three fifteen, West walked to the school bus stop at the end of the long drive to meet Alexa. He was early but he'd been distracted since Gracie had left this morning and needed to take a walk.

The quarter-mile trek had done him good, and he knew Alexa liked having him meet her on the days when she didn't have track practice or some other after-school event. Otherwise, she would have said she was too old to have her dad meet the bus. Sometimes she didn't say a word on the way to the cabin or gave one-word answers to his questions. *How was your day? Fine. Was it pizza day? Yes. How'd your oral report go? Good.*

He stood near the main road by the Heartland Hollows sign, listening for the telltale whoosh. There were a few honks in greeting and waves to him as drivers passed. And then, finally, the long yellow bus with its flashing lights and stop sign swinging out.

Alexa came down the steps and jumped off. He wanted to scoop her into a hug but he'd learned that was a no-go while middle schoolers were watching out the window.

Her long burnished-brown hair was in a low ponytail down one shoulder, a new style. As was the shimmery lip gloss. She wore a pale pink down jacket, jeans and the fuzzy brown boots that all her friends had too. Everyone said she was his mini me, the coloring and her blue eyes especially. He loved her so much that sometimes it took his breath. West had always been a committed person—to his job, to people in his life, to all his responsibilities, but fatherhood, with all the depths of emotion, had been the guiding force of his life these past twelve years. The past *ten*, particularly, since he'd been widowed. And was raising his child on his own.

Everything he did, he did with his daughter in mind, and that their relationship was changing—which he knew was as it should be—was taking some serious getting used to. Gone were days of Alexa sharing her every thought. Now he was lucky if she gave her opinion of dinner. *Fine. Good. Okay...* A few days ago, he'd picked her up from a sleepover with her two best friends, and as the girls giggled away in whispers as they hugged goodbye, the host mom had said to him, *Sometimes it's like they're still little girls, and other times they're like teenagers with secrets. I'm learning as I go.* He'd nodded with a hearty *me, too*, and could have stood there talking about exactly that for hours.

"Good day?" he asked Alexa with a smile as they started up the long drive.

"I guess," she said, eyes straight ahead. Earbuds in.

"So I've got some news about the ranch."

He had no doubt his daughter would be thrilled with

what he was about to say. She might even jump up and down. She'd like going from the foreman's daughter to the owner's daughter. Even *co*-owner's daughter.

She turned to him and pulled out her earbuds. "News? Like what?" She looked nervous. When Bo died, she hadn't asked what would happen now, if they'd be leaving the ranch, if the new owner would bring in his own foreman—a question that had kept him up the past week. Bo hadn't it brought it up in his final months, let alone final days, and West certainly hadn't. Out of respect for Bo's privacy, maybe. West had *wanted* to know, but he'd figured there'd be a lawyer involved, and he'd been right about that. What he'd never entertained, not even in a daydream while out on the range, was that Bo would leave the place to him.

He'd thought a lot about that today—how he'd never imagined Bo would do that. Despite the lack of family or close friends. Who had Bo had besides West? No one.

Why hadn't West assumed or even considered that Bo would leave the Heartland Hollows to him? Especially because Bo knew West loved the place as much as Bo did, had been a part of it from the week Bo had bought the ranch.

His late wife's face came to mind. He'd lost Jenny ten years ago. A long time. Maybe he hadn't even realized how that loss had changed him. *You stopped expecting*, West thought suddenly. *Stopped expecting life to go on as it was. Stopped expecting your beloved daughter to have her mother.*

Started expecting bad things to happen to good peo-

ple. He'd been bracing himself for the worst these past ten years, his shoulders always tensed. That wasn't any way to live. When his phone rang at times when his daughter wasn't beside him or fast asleep safe in bed, his heart would race until the call turned out be a ranch hand reporting a sick calf or Alexa's grandparents asking about having her stay for two weeks over the summer. The ole other shoe could and would drop. On his head.

It struck West that he had to change. For Alexa's sake. Maybe one of the reasons she'd gone total tween and pulled away from him these past months was because he wasn't a "fun dad" like some of her friends seemed to have. Easygoing. *Riley's father said she could go on sleepover, so why can't I?* His response, *Because the host's parents are away for the weekend and no adults will be supervising* was not a good enough answer for Alexa. She'd sulked the entire weekend.

There were things that were nonnegotiable, of course, like that. No parents home, no sleepover. But West had always been more worried about what *could* happen than about living life to the fullest. Didn't he want the latter for his child?

Luckily, Alexa had been asserting away. Making her case. Standing up for herself. Sometimes he had to put his parental foot down, but sometimes she'd make him realize he was being too protective and he'd back down.

It was hard on him, but good for her.

They were making their way and would be fine. He did believe that.

Then last week, Bo's death had gutted him all over again. Opened a decade-old wound that had healed with time and life and his daughter waking up every morning, bacon always getting her out of bed, no matter her mood. For West, wanting to lighten the hell up was just about impossible right now.

Once West had made the funeral arrangements, he'd posted a public announcement in the *Brewer County Gazette* that anyone who would like to gather at the ranch house from 12:00 to 1:00 p.m. to pay their respects was welcome. Several local ranchers and vendors and store owners had come, a few asking outright if West knew what would become of the ranch. Even then it hadn't occurred to him that Bo would leave it to him.

Bo's attorney, who West had never met until the funeral, had pulled him aside at the reception to let him know that West should continue on in his role as foreman until the reading of the will. That hadn't given him any clues about what was forthcoming. *You should have had more faith in Bo, realized what you meant to him,* he thought now. He glanced at Alexa, who'd stopped in her tracks, waiting for him to tell her the big news.

Never ever forget what you mean to this girl, he told himself. *No matter what the tween and teen years bring.*

West gave Alexa's hand a squeeze and then explained to her about the reading of the will this morning. The part about him inheriting half the Heartland Hollows Ranch.

"What!" she shrieked, her eyes lighting up with absolute joy. "Are you serious?"

He nodded. "One hundred percent serious."

She truly did start jumping up and down. "I can't believe it, Daddy!"

Daddy. She rarely called him that these days. He was always Dad now. Except when she was sick or feeling crummy emotionally. Or, apparently, very happy.

"I always knew deep down that Bo cared about us very much," he said. "It was a big surprise and I was very moved."

"You took care of him the last bunch of months," she said, eyeing him. "He knew *you* cared about him too."

Oh, Alexa. Sweet, smart, compassionate girl. He gave her hand another squeeze.

Alexa stopped twirling and looked at him. "Wait, you said we inherited *half* the ranch. Who is getting the other half? How does that work?"

He didn't want to talk to Alexa about the details of baby Liam's inheritance until he had more information. He could see her texts flying now to her friends:

Hey guys, a baby inherited the other half of my dad's ranch! Isn't that wild!

Oh, the speculation and gossip—from middle schoolers with a fun story to mention, to sharing it with their parents, and soon it would be all over town.

"A very nice woman named Gracie Dawson and her six-month-old baby have the other half," he said. "They'll move into the main house and we'll stay in ours since it's so perfect for us."

"Wait—Dawson like the Dawson Family Guest Ranch?" she asked as they resumed walking. The ranch was famed in Bear Ridge, especially because it was run by six siblings and there were many Dawson relatives in town.

"Yup," he said. "She's a cousin."

"I like babies," she said. "They're so cute and have huge cheeks."

West smiled. "You were super cute and had giant cheeks. And you were a great baby. Never fussed. Napped like a champ. Slept through the night early."

Alexa laughed. "I hope the ranch baby will be like that or I might hear it crying from our cabin. Boy or girl?"

"Boy. His name is Liam."

"There are four Liams in my grade. Do you think they'll like the ranch house?"

"It's a really nice house."

She nodded. "I'm glad we're staying in our house. I love our cabin. I know we call it that, but it feels like a real house, a fairy-tale house. And I love my room."

He'd worked hard on that room, transforming the door into an archway and painted pink and purple. Secret nooks and crannies and window seats. He'd expected her to be glad they were staying put. Over the years, he'd renovated both the inside and outside of their "cabin" and it had major curb appeal and the "cool" factor.

"So what's the other owner like?" she asked as the house came into view. They turned onto the path toward their cabin.

"She's very nice. And she seems like a great mom. Loving and doting. It was nice watching her and her baby son—"

Alexa's face fell. She bit her lip and seemed unsure for a moment, then he saw her eyes glistening. Before he could say a word she took off for the cabin, throwing open the door and racing in.

His heart dropped and he exhaled hard. He'd spoken without thinking, something he rarely did with his daughter.

She was twelve years old and couldn't even remember her mother.

Great, loving, doting moms were a sore point. Sometimes, Alexa was absolutely fine, like on sleepovers or at a track meet with loving moms all over the place. And sometimes, the fact that she'd lost her mother would descend on her in a way that sucked the air of her lungs.

He didn't rush after her. There were times, and he wasn't always sure when, that he had to give her a little space. To let her process her emotions. When he arrived at the cabin, he noticed she hadn't stopped to take off her coat. Which meant she was upset.

Upstairs, he found her bedroom door closed. He knocked and called her name. No reply.

"Alexa? It's Dad."

Still no reply.

He opened the door slowly and peeked in. She wasn't in bed under the covers. He found her under the purple "cave" he'd built out from a window. She sat on the long cushion with her legs scrunched up to her chest, arms around them, facing outside.

"Honey," he said gently. "Did it hurt when I talked about the new co-owner being a mom?"

He figured he'd better make sure that was what had upset her.

She didn't respond, which meant the answer was yes. Otherwise, she would have snapped a no.

He stood just a few inches from her and leaned a hip against the wall. "I miss her, too," he said. He'd met Jenny Newland in the cafeteria of the ranch he'd worked at before Heartland Hollows. She was the short-order cook and made great chili. Many of the single cowboys had had a crush on her, but he'd won her heart. They'd been married just a little over two years before the accident—which felt like both yesterday and a hundred years ago at the same time. "I know it hurts that you don't remember your mother. But what you should always know is that she loved you so much, Lex. You made her so happy. She used to watch you sleep, just to watch you breathe. She'd sigh in completely contentment and say she couldn't imagine ever being happier."

Alexa shifted slightly but didn't lift her head and he could see her reaching up a hand to swipe away tears. "She wanted to name me Alexa, right?" She turned then, looking up at him.

He moved over to the cave and knelt down, then squeezed in next to her on the seat and put his arm around her. "Yup. She said it had always been her favorite name since she was little and wished it were *her* name."

He must have told her that a thousand times over the years, but it always made her smile, as it did now, a spirit coming back into her eyes.

"There are no Alexas in my grade," she said, which had been the case since kindergarten. "There are two Alexandras and one Alexis. But no Alexas. I like that I'm the only one. I guess I'll text Riley and Lauren and tell them we own the ranch now. I still can barely believe it."

He kissed the top of her head. *Give her space*, he told himself. "I know. Same here. I'll make Nutella-banana slices. Come down if you want some before I eat them all." It was her favorite snack.

"'K, Dad."

He put a hand on her shoulder and left the room, letting out a deep breath once he was on the stairs. *Just when I think I don't have this*, he sent heavenward, *that I keep getting it wrong, it works out*. That was advice everyone had given him back when he'd lost Jenny, when he'd break down with friends, even Jenny's parents, at how he was going to do this alone.

You love Alexa, his in-laws would say, *you're a good guy, and those two things will guide you. You'll be fine...*

Though sometimes he felt so alone, alone in terms of parenting, that he'd start thinking about getting remarried, finding someone who'd make a great stepmother, a great life partner. Ten years and none of his dates had gone anywhere. Mostly his fault, he knew. For this or that reason.

He sighed and headed downstairs and into the kitchen.

Gracie Dawson came to mind. He'd liked how she'd fiercely defended her position at Heartland Hollows, that she wouldn't be a silent partner, that she'd be working the ranch. He had no doubt she'd protect her son's interests first and foremost. As should be the case. He also liked how forthright she was, whether about not knowing Bo or not understanding how her baby's father had walked out on her and their baby-to-be. There was an honesty to her. And she let herself be vulnerable around others, something that had always been hard for him.

Alexa, too, would like Gracie Dawson, he had no doubt of that. She'd enjoy having a woman around since there was only one part-time cowgirl and her hours had never matched with when Alexa was home from school.

As he opened the fridge in search of the Nutella, he had an awareness that their lives were about to change. He just wasn't sure exactly *how*.

What a day, Gracie thought as she stood beside her mom at the kitchen counter in their family home. They were making dinner—soft chicken tacos with a side of black beans. Linda Dawson had just finished shredding the spicy, fragrant chicken, and Gracie was pouring salsa into a bowl. She was distracted, though, her gaze more often out the window than on her dinner prep. It was just past 6:00 p.m. and the sun had set over an hour ago, snow flurries caught in the illumination of the front yard lights.

She could feel her mom glancing at her and tried to focus. Gracie moved to the stove, adding a little cumin into the pot of simmering beans, but her thoughts kept returning to the events of the morning. She froze for a second with her hand on the chili powder—had she already stirred some in?

She sighed and figured better safe than too spicy.

Her life had been turned upside down in a snap. In the very brief reading of a will. The will of a man she'd never met, didn't know, had never heard of.

Then there was West Calhoun. And the hour at the Heartland Hollows Ranch and all they'd discussed, all they'd *disclosed*. Gracie had shared more about herself to West in that hour in the ranch house kitchen than she had with anyone in years beside her mom and grandmother and her best friend Miranda, who was out of town till after the holidays.

He was either *that* easy to talk to or she'd been off center because of how her life had suddenly changed. Her baby had inherited half a multimillion-dollar ranch. Gracie had been tasked with managing it for him until he became of age. They would move into the lovely ranch house. She still couldn't believe any of it. Then again, it was hard to process when she couldn't even figure out her connection to Bo Bixby. *Liam's* connection.

She recalled how West had held Liam to try to

soothe him when he'd gotten so fussy. If she'd worried that the man had any secret plans to keep her in the dark, despite what he'd said, his gentle, tender way with her baby son, the little interloper in West's life, spoke volumes.

Liam had fussed the whole way home but dabbing a cold, damp washcloth on his gums and then chilling his pacifier had seemed do the trick. He was content in his bouncer in the corner with a full, happy belly from his first try of scrambled eggs now that he'd started solids, watching the dangling mobile of little pastel animals spin gently.

"Taco time," her mom said with a smile, using tongs to move the lightly grilled tortillas onto two plates. "I want mine with the works." They built their tacos with the base of chicken, which smelled delicious, then added their toppings, Gracie going for lettuce, cheese, a little sour cream and the salsa. It was just the two of them for dinner since her dad had taken her grandmother to a combo bean supper and bingo event at the town hall.

They brought their plates over to the table and sat, taking bites and watching Liam gaze at his mobile. Her mom was quiet and Gracie could see she was still ruminating on the big news she'd come home with this morning—no doubt the new living arrangements. Gracie and Liam would be moving out. When they'd started making dinner, her mother had put on an apron, as she always did, but Gracie had noticed it was one she'd made for her mom when she was nine years old, from a kit involving painted handprints and glitter.

Linda Dawson liked having her only child and grandchild living at home and tomorrow they'd be gone.

"I know the Heartland Hollows Ranch is just ten minutes from here, but still," her mom said with a frown. "I love having you and Liam here. So do Dad and Gram."

On her way home from the ranch earlier, Gracie had assumed that her parents and grandmother would move with her. The ranch house was large, and West had mentioned there were four bedrooms. The Dawsons could each have their own room, including a nursery for Liam. But then she remembered that all the bedrooms were on the second floor, which was a problem. The family house, which Gracie had grown up in, was a ranch style with three bedrooms on the first level. Both her parents and grandmother had said that stairs, particularly a steep set like at the ranch, would be too much on them and they were comfortable here. It had been home for a long time.

"I like that you told him what's what," her mother said, then took another bite of her taco. "If he's expecting a silent partner who'll be shopping all day, oh, is he gonna be surprised."

Gracie smiled. "He didn't look particularly nervous when I told him I plan to be fully involved. I know I *just* met him, but I have a good feeling about him. There's just something trustworthy about West Calhoun."

"I'm glad to hear that. He'll see what you're made of your first day there." Her mom took a bite of the beans then raised an eyebrow. "I think something's missing. Chili power, maybe."

Gracie laughed. "Sorry. I was distracted when I was adding the spices."

Her mom put her fork down and turned toward Gracie, reaching out her arms to grasp her shoulders. "Of course you were. Today was a big day. Tomorrow will be bigger. But you know your way around a ranch. You'll do just fine. Twenty years from now, Liam will be thanking you for taking such good care of his interests."

Twenty years from now. The thought made her shiver. One of Linda Dawson's oft-used phrases was *The days are long but the years are short.* Gracie wasn't ready to think of her baby boy all grown up. But she absolutely would take good care of his inheritance. "I don't know what I'd do without your support."

"I'm always here, honey," her mom said, taking another bite of the beans, despite the missing chili powder. "So, still no ideas on Liam's connection to Bo Bixby?" her mom asked.

"I can't think of anything. How can that be? I keep going back to the link having to do with Liam's father. But Harry said he had no family after his mom died when he was eighteen. And West said that Bo had no family either. I thought that maybe Harry had been a cowboy on the Heartland Hollows, but West would have recognized his name immediately when I brought it up in the lawyer's office. And it wouldn't explain why Bo would single out Harry's baby and not the five other employees since two have kids. Nothing about this adds up."

"I've been trying to think too. You know I'm kind of

a busybody and like to keep up with what's going on in town. The name Bo Bixby didn't jump out at me when I was looking in the obituaries for who passed that *you* might have known. But once you told me it was him, I remembered how he was the talk at Hair Flair for weeks after he bought the Heartland Hollows. Single. Handsome. Early fifties, then, I believe. I knew a few divorced ladies who planned to bring over welcome baskets or stop by to ask advice for buying a small ranch."

"Did he date? West made him seem like a real loner."

"I recall seeing him around town with a few women over the years. A date here and there. But never anyone on his arm and never the same woman. Maybe he was just one of those confirmed bachelor types. Or he'd been divorced and widowed and was done with romance." She shrugged.

Gracie pushed beans around on her plate. "So he gets diagnosed with cancer, knows he doesn't have much time, and decides to leave half his ranch to a baby he never met. Why? Why? Why?"

"Dad, Gram and I were talking about little else all afternoon. We couldn't come up with anything. You never met Bo. He didn't have family—so Harry wasn't a relative. So *what* is Liam's connection to him? It's a total mystery, hon."

It sure was.

They gave up on that connection, at least for tonight, and finished their dinner, then had chocolate–chocolate chip ice cream for dessert. Her mom's sister called to chat, so Gracie excused herself to start packing. Earlier this afternoon the attorney had emailed paperwork to sign and information about the ranch; she'd carefully read the documents and signed, saving the history and financials of Heartland Hollows for her bedtime reading. That the ranch was in excellent shape was evident.

In her room, she settled Liam into his playpen while she got out two big suitcases. Gracie wasn't exactly a clotheshorse, though she did have a collection of footwear for ranch work, so packing wouldn't be difficult. She'd bring some family photos and some personal things that would make the ranch house feel more familiar. She certainly wouldn't charge in and start changing anything; she'd go slowly, get the lay of the land.

And of West Calhoun.

As she packed, she made a mental note of things she'd need to take care of. She'd already called her cousin Daisy at the Dawson Family Guest Ranch and explained that a new venture had suddenly come up and that Gracie had so appreciated the Dawsons giving her work when she knew they didn't even have openings. Of course, Daisy had been curious about the new venture, but Gracie had just said she'd be at the Heartland Hollows Ranch and left out the details since she wanted details *herself* first. Daisy had been excited for her and mentioned that she knew the foreman and he was a top-notch guy. Gracie was glad to hear *that*. She definitely already had a good feeling about West, yes, but she'd been wrong about people in the past. Her cousin's thumbs-up did a lot to set her mind at ease about everything she was about to walk into.

Her dad and grandmother had returned, so her mom

came in to get her grandbaby so they could spend some time with him and get him ready for bed. They wanted to make this last night having him here special. Her dad and gram had stopped in the general store, which had a gift section and holiday department, and they'd bought Liam a tiny cowboy hat since he was now a full-fledged rancher. They plopped it on his head, which he did not seem to mind—a good sign for his future, they decided—and they all took a hundred photos.

She loved her family so much. It would be hard to be away from them, but they were an easy drive if she ever got stressed or needed a hug.

She spent the next half hour packing, then settled in on her bed with her homework. She'd be prepared for her first day as co-owner's interest-keeper. And for West Calhoun.

After dinner—West's specialty, lasagna and his version of garlic knots—he and Alexa headed to the main house to make it welcoming for the new residents. He hadn't been sure Alexa would be interested in that, but she'd said it was perfect timing since she'd finished her math homework. She'd pulled out the earbuds and leapt off the sofa.

Alexa was full of questions on the way. *Is the baby a crier? Do you think Gracie will ask me to babysit?* She knew several girls at school who were mother's helpers, but for preschool and older. Would she have to change a diaper? She wrinkled up her nose at that. West told her they could certainly bring up that she'd be interested in a "job" as a mother's helper.

He'd glanced at her, unsure if the subject would bring her down, but she remained excited and curious.

In the house, which he'd paid a cleaning service a small fortune for a rush deep-clean after Gracie had left, even he noticed the fresh scent and sparkle to the wood floors and freshly vacuumed rugs. Not a bit of dust anywhere. The country kitchen, which Bo had updated a few years ago with quartz counters, an island, deep blue cabinets and stainless-steel appliances, gleamed.

"Alexa," he said as they headed into the living room, "how about you go through the foyer and living room and fill up these boxes with anything that feels personal to Bo. Gracie will have a nicely furnished house but she'll want to make it her and Liam's. With their own touches."

"I'm on it!" she said, looking around.

He smiled and put together the moving boxes, grabbing duct tape from a "junk" drawer in the kitchen to make the bottoms sturdy.

He'd already packed up Bo's clothes while Alexa had been at school. Bo hadn't had an extensive wardrobe, just the usual ranch wear, from casual to dressier, a few suits, various footwear, and the outerwear a rancher needed for Wyoming winters. Bo had four cowboy hats, two for the range and two Stetsons. West had kept them—all he'd taken from the house. Bo had never worn a watch or any jewelry. West had also earlier cleared out the three bathrooms, one en suite with the primary, one in the hallway, and one downstairs, of all Bo's medications and toiletries, his razors and shaving cream. He'd instructed the cleaning team to strip all the beds and wash everything, from pillows to comforters—which was worth the extra cost.

Now he went through the primary suite's bedside tables, sending a quick apology heavenward for the intrusion. He wouldn't be surprised to find them empty.

One was. The side without the pile of books atop it and the coaster. He added the books—a Stephen King novel, a nonfiction tome on animal husbandry, and the Bible, which Bo had asked West to read certain scriptures from the last month of his life. Always the same ones. About sorrow, the brokenhearted and crushed spirits.

You can talk to me, Bo, West had said many times in different variations, his voice always cracking at the man's bedside.

I know it, Bo would always respond and pat his hand, and that would be that.

Bo had taken his secrets with him.

One drawer of the bedside table was empty. The bottom one had a small wooden box with engraving on it. *Bixby*. Again, West sent up a *Sorry*, then tried to open the box, but he realized it was locked; there was a small keyhole. He looked around the drawer for a key but there was nothing. He pulled out his key ring and jammed the edge of his cabin key in between the top and bottom—and it gave. He wedged it open.

Empty.

Huh. That was weird. A *locked* box with his name engraved on it in his bedside table drawer. But containing absolutely nothing. Maybe something had been in it, something important. But why lock an empty box? As usual, lots of questions, no answers.

As he came downstairs with the box and books in the tote bag he'd brought with him, he found Alexa studying a small statue on the console in the foyer. She titled her head left then right. It was a gray stone gargoyle, about four inches high, a cross between Yoda and a monster—with wings.

She turned when she heard his footsteps on the stairs. "I don't think Gracie would want this to be the first thing she sees when she comes in every day, you know? It might scare the baby."

He smiled. "Good thinking. There's a nice oval bowl on the mantel that would look great in that spot. She could toss her keys on it, the baby's pacifier."

Her face lit up that she was right about the gargoyle. She took the statue over to the box and wrapped it with the newspaper he'd stuffed in, then set it inside, returning with the bowl. She placed it just so, centered with the ornate mirror above the table. "Much better, Dad."

"Agreed."

She was now looking in the mirror and fussing with her hair, so to give her some privacy, he went into the kitchen and looked around. He'd gone through the cabinets and drawers earlier and figured everything could stay, from flatware and cookware to plates and mugs to can openers and spatulas. Nothing was posted to the fridge with magnets, which wasn't a surprise given that Bo had everything on his phone, from his calendar to numbers for his staff and vendors.

When he returned to the living room, Alexa was

looking around as if making sure she didn't miss anything. He eyed the two boxes and saw she'd filled up about a quarter of one box. It seemed clear she hadn't missed a thing. In the living room and hallways there were no photos, except interesting shots of cattle, the ranch itself, from the sign atop the entry gates to the Heartland Hollows Ranch staff. Only two photos were left on the mantel. One of the first herd Bo had bought ten years ago, Black Angus, the gray barn and mountains in the distance. And another of the ranch staff, which included him and Bo by the gate of the Heartland Hollows. There had been two other photos, both of West and Alexa—when she was six and had just lost her first tooth and more recently on her twelfth birthday. But Alexa had put those in the box.

When West had started coming to the house to take care of Bo, he'd been surprised—and deeply touched—by those photos. Surprised because Bo hadn't really paid attention to Alexa all these years; he always got her a kind and generous gift for her birthday and Christmas, and any staff member with a child received a huge Easter basket from the general store. But otherwise, Bo hadn't engaged with Alexa or with the two children of two of the staffers who'd come "help" out Daddy every now and then. Any time Alexa would cross paths before Bo had been diagnosed, he would say hello to her, acknowledge her presence, but he never asked about school or what her weekend plans might be. West had just figured that Bo had no interest or patience for kids. It certainly spoke to why he'd never had a family of his own.

Many times West had been in Bo's home office, which had an entrance from outside that staff used, but he'd never stepped foot in the house itself through the front door until Bo had gotten sick. Days after Bo's diagnosis, West had been invited into the house. Bo had sat him down in the living room with a glass of scotch, and West had seen the photos of him and Alexa on the mantel and had suddenly understood, with absolute clarity, that he hadn't known Bo Bixby at all. He'd thought he had, that still waters ran deep and all that. But he never in a million years would have expected Bo to have family photos of him and his daughter displayed.

"I was right to leave all this stuff, right, Dad?" Alexa asked, turning slowly and pointing in all directions. "There were pictures of us on the mantel, but they seemed personal, not like the staff photo. I don't know why exactly."

A lump formed in his throat. "Because he thought of us as family," he said, slinging an arm around her as a memory overtook him. Bo had had a sweet tooth and particularly liked M&M's. After mentioning that to Alexa in Bo's final month, she'd left a family-size bag of fun-size plain and peanut with a Post-it attached that said, *To Bo, hope you're feeling good today—Alexa Calhoun*. When West had brought it to Bo, he'd looked at it for a long moment and said, *Sweet girl*, his voice frail in those final days. West had had to excuse himself to let it out—the tears that had come falling down his face.

Now, Alexa smiled up at him, a sweet wonder in

her eyes. "I guess he musta, right? Since he left us half the ranch. Is it like that with the Dawson lady?"

"I'm not sure," he said honestly. Supposed strangers or not, Gracie and Bo must have crossed paths somehow. In a big way. They'd figure it out, hopefully tomorrow, so they could forget the big mystery and focus on the day-to-day and the big picture.

West looked around, noting the stately black wrought-iron candlestick holders with the ivory candles on the mantel. The art on the walls. The carvings of cowboys and horses and a framed vintage poster from a long-ago rodeo. He'd leave Gracie to remove anything that didn't suit her. But the furnishings and décor were neutral-Western and the home was warm and welcoming.

"You did a great job making the place nice for Gracie and Liam."

Alexa beamed. They did a final check, declared the house ready for the new co-owners, and drove back home.

A couple of hours later, when he was leaving Alexa's bedroom after a kiss goodnight on the forehead and a *Sweet dreams*, he stopped short by the door. She'd put the gargoyle statue on her desk.

Be still my heart, he thought. He wasn't sure if she'd wanted something special from Bo's house or knew that gargoyles warded off evil spirits, or if she just liked the little statue even if she thought Gracie wouldn't, but the sentiment touched him.

An omen for things to come.

Chapter Four

In the morning, the Dawson family arrived at the Heartland Hollows Ranch in two separate cars, since of course, Gracie and Liam would be staying. In the cargo areas were their suitcases and personal effects, including Liam's crib, which Gracie had spent a good hour taking apart for transport, the changing table, and a small antique dressing table and chair that had been in her family for generations and would instantly make whatever bedroom she took feel more like home.

She wondered where West was right now. Taking inventory in the barn? Out on the range with the cowboys? West had told her that it was a good thing his daughter was twelve and able to be home alone for stretches because he was now always on call.

He's not just the foreman anymore. She understood. As owners, the two of them would always be on call, every day, all day. And night. She could see two cowboys near the big barns up the path and one on horseback in one of the fields with a small herd of cattle. The dusting of snow was gone and the herd could graze, despite the scrubby almost-brown grass.

They got out of their cars, her family slack-jawed as

they stood looking in every direction. They were having the same reaction to the place—and the house—as she had yesterday. *Wow* from everyone. Gracie glanced around for West but she didn't see him. It was Saturday and he was likely home with his daughter in the foreman's cabin, making pancakes and bacon. She smiled at the thought. She was planning on introducing Liam to the joy of pancakes with a little pure maple syrup this weekend.

She was hoping that West would notice the car and come say hello. A warm welcome now that she was officially moving in. Something to take the edge off her nerves, make her feel like she had a friend here. They were business partners, yes. But a personal connection, as they'd made yesterday, would do wonders for her comfort level. Gracie had never been great at change.

She went to the cargo area of her SUV to get her backpack and cross-body purse—and because she wanted to give West a minute to notice they were here and come by.

Not happening, apparently. Maybe he wasn't even home right now. Maybe he'd taken Alexa to breakfast at the diner in town. Maybe he was far out on the range on horseback. Bags in hand, she started up the porch steps since it was cold out and they should get Liam inside. Her dad took the bags, and her mom linked arms with her grandmother for the three-step climb up to the beautiful porch. She'd get a porch swing, for sure. And maybe when Liam was out of the stroller and didn't need two hands to wheel him about, she'd think about adopting a dog. She could just see a pooch snoozing on a bed beside the swing. A cat grooming itself on the railing.

You're making yourself feel at home, she realized with a boost of confidence.

Her dad carried in the two reusable tote bags full of groceries, which her parents had been so thoughtful to pick up for her, everything from her favorite macadamia-nut-flavored coffee and all the fixings to eggs to deli meat, her favorite cheeses, a few different kinds of breads, produce, frozen pizzas and baby food for Liam. They'd added in a huge sack of diapers and baby wipes. She'd go shopping next week to stock the pantry and fridge and freezer, but she was set for now.

Once inside the house, Gracie immediately sensed something was different. It took a few minutes of looking around the living room and kitchen to figure it out—and only because her grandmother said, "The house is so clean!"

That was it. The place was perfectly fine when West had taken her on a tour yesterday, but she could see now that the home *sparkled*—and smelled so fresh. Which meant that he'd somehow cleaned the whole house himself after she'd left or had hired a service—she'd bank on that. The man didn't exactly have free time on his hands. Either way, she was touched. It spoke to the kind of person he was. Thoughtful. Considerate. Went a step farther.

While her father got Liam's bouncer set up by the sliding-glass doors to the deck and settled the baby inside, great-grandma playing a round of peekaboo, Gracie felt a strange sense of *Where am I?*

Nothing was familiar. Nothing felt like hers.

But this was her home now.

"Give it a little time," her mom said, clearly having read her expression. "It's all new."

Gracie nodded. "I still can't believe any of this. Liam owns half the place. We *live* here now. Our entire futures both changed with a few words in a stranger's will."

Her dad was about to say something when there was a knock on the front door.

And now it was Gracie's door to answer. She opened it to find West Calhoun, handsome in a brown leather jacket and brown Stetson, standing on the porch holding on a medium-sized bonsai tree in a beautiful stone pot.

He smiled, and for a second she was mesmerized by the sight of him. As expected, *he* felt familiar and even comforting, if everything else about Heartland Hollows didn't.

"For good luck and good fortune," he said, gesturing at the plant.

She smiled, aware of a flutter of butterflies in her belly. The man *was* thoughtful. "Very nice of you, West. I love it. I think it would look great on the mantel."

He nodded and came in, Gracie shutting the door behind him.

"You must be West," her mother said, coming over and extending her hand. "I'm Linda Dawson and this," she added, pointing to where her husband and mother were sitting on the chairs near the baby bouncer, "is my husband, Larry, and my mother, Dorothea Atwood."

West set the plant on the mantel, and it did look fabulous there, like a beautiful symbol of good fortune indeed. Then he headed over to her dad and grandmother, and they all shook his hands, Gracie's grandmother taking both of West's in hers.

West squatted to say hi to Liam, which had Gracie's *heart* fluttering. "Welcome to your new home, young rancher."

Oh, my. Gracie could see the swoony look her mom and grandmother were giving each other.

West stood. "Can I help unload the vehicles?"

Now, her mother and grandmother were practically fanning themselves. Gracie hid her smile. She herself might be getting used to the man's kindness, his generosity. But she'd never take either for granted.

"Sure can," her dad said, making small talk toward the door about college sports and the rodeo. She could tell her father liked what he'd seen of West so far, offers to help, sweetly chatting up his new baby partner. Still, Larry Dawson was clearly sizing him up. For all her dad knew, West was buttering up the family so they'd not look at him—and his actions concerning the ranch, the business of the ranch—too closely.

Well, they would. It was Gracie's duty and she'd take that very seriously. No matter how nice, how trustworthy, West Calhoun seemed.

And she knew that poor West was about to hit by a barrage of questions once they were outside. Fine with Gracie. Her dad leaned toward blunt and maybe he'd think to ask West things she hadn't thought of about the logistics of owning the ranch together.

Gracie scooped up Liam, and she and her mom went upstairs to pick out a nursery. This would be the first time he had his own room. For the past six months, they'd shared Gracie's childhood bedroom. With her new salary, she'd be able to buy what she always wistfully walked past at the big-box store on trips to Brewer, from an exersaucer for Liam to the classic children's books she'd love to have on his bookshelf. She was so used to being frugal and counting her pennies, she was sure it would take her some time to get used to what her life had suddenly become.

The room she had in mind for the nursery was the second bedroom off the hallway. Something about the light coming in from the windows, the square shape. It felt homey and cozy. Her mom agreed, and by the time her father and West had arrived with the deconstructed crib, she knew just where she wanted things placed. West started putting the crib together on his own, her parent giving each other *Isn't that nice?* glances. As West worked, her parents went downstairs to cart up the crib mattress, her grandmother exploring the rooms on the second level.

"I appreciate all your help," Gracie said to him as he turned a hex wrench on a bolt.

He ran a hand through his thick dark hair, his Stetson left behind on the console table in the foyer. "No problem at all. I've done this before." He looked up at her and smiled, and she was struck again by how good-looking he was. She'd been aware before, of course, but…that smile. He was done with the crib in a quarter of the amount of time it would have taken her, and he zipped back down to get the changing table.

Her parents came up with the mattress, and when they had the sheets on, with the moon-stars pattern in soft yellow and silver, the crib looked so welcoming by the window against the robin's-egg blue walls. Her grandmother gave it her seal of approval.

West and her father returned with the changing table and got it set up across the room. Once she had the white terry-cloth pad on it, a basket of diapers and ointment and corn starch on the shelf below, the room looked like a nursery with just those pieces of furniture. And the baby in the bouncer, of course. *This is your room, Liam Hurley Dawson. This is your house.*

"Well, I'll leave you to get settled, Gracie," West said. "If you need anything at all, don't hesitate to call or text. I'm right down the road." He turned to her family. "Great to meet you all."

They fussed and clasped his hand again, and then he was gone.

"I like him," her grandmother said with a nod.

"Me, too," her mom said.

"Nice guy," her dad put in with a nod.

He's special, she thought suddenly with a jot. *Unusual.* And a little too easy on the eyes. Her thoughts drifted to his face and the way his muscles had moved under his Henley shirt as he'd put the crib together.

A harmless crush from afar on her handsome, gallant co-owner was fine. As long as she kept it to that. She doubted that would be an issue. Not when her trust level in men and romance were at an all-time low, thanks to the father of her baby.

Even a hint of attraction between her and West Calhoun could do a lot of damage down the road. And given that she was tasked with managing Liam's inheritance, she'd make sure nothing threatened her child's legacy.

West stood outside the cattle barn in a brief meeting with the three employees who were working today when he noticed Gracie's parents and grandmother leaving the main house. A quarter mile away, he couldn't see them well, but there was Gracie on the porch with Liam in a baby carrier strapped to her down coat. The trio walked toward their vehicle, then her mother turned back and ran up the porch steps, wrapping Gracie and Liam in a dual hug. Linda Dawson hurried to the SUV, and as it drove away, Gracie stayed where she was, hand up in a wave toward the vehicle.

Something in how she stood there, watching even after the SUV disappeared from view, told him she felt alone right now. Nervous probably. She had arrived into a whole new world, new people, new worries, and her responsibilities must feel huge. Her family had clearly been a comfort while she was moving in and getting settled the past couple of hours, and now they were gone.

He itched to do something for her, something more than a housewarming plant, to let her know she had a friend in him. They were scheduled to meet in an hour and a half for her tour of the ranch and to go over ownership and logistics. He'd do what he could to set her mind at ease about how overwhelming this all was. He felt it himself, but at least he knew Heartland Hollows inside and out and had been part of this place for ten years. For Gracie, nothing was familiar except ranching itself, but that was big. She had an immediate comfort level. She'd be just fine in a week.

He'd emailed the entire staff about the new ownership at Heartland Hollows and that nothing would change. They'd all emailed back their congrats with not only various positive emojis, from a smiley face in a cowboy hat to fire symbol, but a few heartfelt lines about their appreciation of him. He'd been so moved by their responses that he'd actually felt a warmth in his chest.

When parenthood could make him second-guess himself at least once a day, that he had it right on the work front meant a lot.

He hadn't mentioned to the staff that that the co-owner they hadn't yet met was a six-month-old who was cutting his first baby tooth. Gracie was his partner until Liam came of age, so there was no need to throw a strange story into the mix. Word would spread and until Liam and Gracie figured out why Bo had left the ranch to a baby, they'd keep that detail to themselves. He let the Saturday staff—a cowboy and two ranch hands—know that he'd be walking Gracie around the ranch in about an hour and if they saw the two of them, to come over to meet her.

His meeting with the crew disbanded and he put out a few fires, everything from a possibly ill bull to equipment issues. He stopped at his cabin to wash up and down a cup of coffee, then headed over to the main house for his meeting with Gracie.

He knocked, and when she opened the door with a smile, he was struck by how pretty she was. That had been clear in the attorney's office yesterday morning, but he'd been so distracted then that he hadn't paid attention to how green her eyes were and her delicate features, except for the plush, pink-red lips. Her long blond hair was wavy past her shoulders. She wore a sweater and jeans again, and socks with little smiling cows on them. She looked like she belonged here.

He grinned. "I like your socks. My daughter has those in every color. From the general store."

She nodded with a smile. "Don't tell anyone, but so do I." She held open the door fully and he came in.

"Can I tell Alexa? She'll know you're a kindred spirit."

Her smile lit up her face. "*Only* Alexa."

He laughed. "Deal."

He almost extended his hand just so he could feel hers in his. He'd have to watch his physical attraction to her, keep it under the surface. That shouldn't be too difficult, given how important it was to keep their relationship all business. Friendly, fine. Anything beyond that, no.

"I'm excited to meet her."

"I'm sure that'll happen sometime later today. She'll be at a friend's most of the day but can't wait to meet you and her new baby neighbor. So I thought we'd start off with a tour of the ranch. We can talk on the way."

"Sounds good. Liam loves the chest carrier, especially now that he faces out to see everything. He's in his playpen. I'll get him bundled up and off we'll go."

He stepped in a bit further as she went into the living room. He noticed she'd added some framed photos to the mantel, of her and Liam, her and her parents. One of Liam sat right next to the bonsai, his tiny partner with a big-cheeked smile.

She'd hung some artwork, too, and some of her things were scattered about the entry and living room. The place had a warmer vibe now. He waited a beat, expecting to feel that sense of loss about Bo's memory getting farther and father away from him with each day, each change. Didn't happen. Maybe it was the feeling of life that now infused the ranch house. Winter gear on the coatrack signifying that people came and went instead of remained inside.

Dammit, now that *did* send a burst of sadness through him.

She was back in a minute with the baby in his little snowsuit in her arms, and immediately his thoughts were with her, on this family of two. "Would you mind holding him for me while I get my coat on?"

As he took Liam, the little guy stared at West's face intently. The big, curious blue eyes then moved to the collar of West's leather barn coat, which he grabbed with quite a grip. "Howdy, partner. And I mean that literally."

Gracie laughed. "I could use some levity on that subject, so thanks." She put on her silver-gray down coat, then pulled on her wool hat. In less than thirty seconds, she had the baby carrier on and latched, which amazed him. It had always taken him a full five minutes. He slipped Liam inside for her, and realized he was standing way too close to Gracie. So close that if he looked up, he would be in kissing distance. The sudden awareness of that stopped him cold. Maybe keeping his attraction in check wouldn't be as easy as he'd thought.

He stepped back and smiled at his tiny partner to diffuse the moment. If Gracie had noticed *any* of that, it didn't show on her face.

Unexpected, he thought, slightly shaken. The first couple of years after he was widowed, he'd never noticed women. Year three, he'd spot long, straight, dark hair in the supermarket or the park and he'd freeze at how similar it was to his late wife's. By the fourth year, he was always surprised when he found women attractive, drawn by a dimple or a smile. He'd started dating when even his late wife's parents told him it was time, that they knew he'd choose a woman with the wonderful qualities of their daughter who'd make an excellent stepmother for Alexa.

He'd sat with that a long time and then had started dating, a few weeks with a woman here, a few months there, but no one got inside him. The past five years, he'd dated plenty, sometimes actively looking. He'd come up empty. Top of his list was *Would make a great stepmother*. If someone checked that box, the next box would go unchecked, whether about chemistry or attraction or anything remotely in common.

His last date was two months ago, when he'd

thought he'd needed to get out, needed a break—if just for a couple of hours—from his heartache over Bo getting frailer and frailer, getting sicker and sicker, before his eyes. A few clicks on the dating app and the next night he'd been sitting across from a pretty redhead at the bar of an Italian restaurant in Brewer. And then she'd said, *So you have a twelve-year-old daughter? Ugh, the worst, right? I was a nightmare to my parents from twelve on. Still am, lol! But if we get serious we'll just keep that part of our lives separate. Me, dealing with a rude preteen? No thanks.* And then she laughed like any of that was funny. He'd immediately told her that they weren't a match and that he had to be getting back to his daughter. She'd scoffed a *Good luck out there* at him and that was that.

His dates were either just okay, uncomfortable due lack of chemistry that made even small talk feel awkward, or left him burning to leave as soon as possible, like the last one.

When Bo was diagnosed and had actually shared that with him, West had known that Bo understood that he not only needed help but *wanted* it. From someone he felt close to. And that West would step into the role of caring for him throughout treatment. That had meant a lot to West. Bo might have been reticent and guarded and closed off, but he'd clearly known he could count on West. And the man had wanted West beside him during the vulnerable time of serious illness.

West had been all too glad to push dating off his list of things to do. But a couple of months ago, Bo had said, *You should find your person.* West had tried to say he had his hands full with the ranch and Alexa, and dating was a drag, but Bo had shaken his head and said that love was something to aspire to, giving and receiving, and then changed the subject. It was a rare instance of Bo saying anything to West beyond *How's Alexa these days?*

West had thought that having a wonderful woman in his life would be a good thing, particularly someone to turn to with his deep sadness about Bo. Or, at the very least, he'd have a couple of hours break from the pain. But he'd gotten that doozy for the last date. And his previous *relationship*, all of two months, which had ended right before Bo had been diagnosed, should have clued him in that finding The One wouldn't be easy. She'd told him he seemed "impenetrable" and if he was going to be so closed off, how would she ever get close? She'd added, *I mean, you've been widowed almost ten years, West.*

He'd wondered long and hard about that—if he was actually like Bo Bixby. Remote. But he knew he wasn't. He was a very present father, maybe even a little too present. Alexa Joy Calhoun would never describe him as impenetrable or remote or closed off. And she might be twelve but she knew him pretty well.

He figured he just couldn't force feelings that weren't there. That was where he'd gone wrong with his last girlfriend, but because she had seemed like she'd make a good stepmother and he was attracted to her, he'd kept seeing her, hoping he'd feel something deep inside his chest. In his heart. But the feelings never materialized. As she'd tried to get closer, he'd pulled farther away. He'd hated that he'd hurt her.

This was the world of dating. And he was done with it for a while. He had too much going on right now. Whether or not that was an excuse, he was using it.

This was why his attraction, on quite a few levels, to Gracie Dawson was so disconcerting. There was that unnamable, untouchable, indescribable *something* about her. Besides how pretty she was, how sexy. There was that instant connection, that feeling, that zap to the nerve endings, that made no sense, given he barely knew her.

She was smart and warm and interesting. Immersed in the world of ranching, like him. A devoted parent, like him. And also like him, she'd been through a lot. He did feel an unusual connection, a serious spark, maybe because of the attraction *and* their unique partnership. They were in this together, long haul.

And, yeah, he had to admit he found her insanely sexy. She had lush curves, full breasts, long legs. Beautiful hair that made him want to run his fingers through it. Green eyes that were hard to look away from. Like right now, when she was telling him how beautiful the land at Heartland Hollows was, how she could just stare out at the pastures and snowcapped evergreens, at the majestic mountains in the distance, and feel easily rooted.

Yes, same here.

This was some *serious*-level attraction.

What made this all okay for him was that she *was* his business partner, so that very naturally meant there could be nothing between them without asking for trouble. And West didn't go around asking for trouble. Maybe he was letting himself actually admit his attraction and *feel* it because it was safe. He'd never act on it.

For the next hour, they walked around the ranch, and he introduced the employees working today. She was warm and friendly to them, and he could see relief on their faces that the new co-boss seemed nice. They fussed over Liam, all declaring him one of the cutest babies they'd ever seen. They didn't even know they were buttering up the *real* boss.

"Ready to head to the office and sit and talk logistics?" he asked as they reached one of the far pastures, a herd grazing on the stubby brownish grass.

"Ready," she said with a smile.

As they walked back to the house, he was so aware of her beside him, taking everything in, asking questions, pointing out things to Liam that had captured her attention, like a skittering twig or a cloud moving across the sky. They went into the house, directly into the office from the outside entrance located to the side. West assured her the door was always locked and she would have the only key. There was a plaque above the doorbell reading Ranch Office, and a small whiteboard protected by a covered overhang in case anyone wanted to leave a note, though the staff mainly communicated by text except when an actual call was warranted if there was an emergency.

"We could hold meetings here as needed, including staff meetings, like Bo did, or we can be less formal and use the barn. Not the red barn, which is mostly decorative and sometimes used as a garage if there's a bad snowstorm forecasted. But the gray barn on the left has a big break room with a sofa and love seat, a round table and chairs, and a refreshments station. Small fridge, coffee maker, fruit and granola bars. I considered it part of my job to keep it stocked."

"That's really nice," she said. "I've worked at ranches where there were no freebies and others, like the Dawson Family Guest Ranch, where there were so many free creature comforts for staff."

He nodded. "Bo believed in treating his employees very well."

"Good. We're both in favor of continuing."

As Gracie went through the office into the living room to get Liam's bouncer and then got him settled into it on the side of the desk, West made coffee at the setup on the credenza along the wall. They sat in the guest chairs across from the big wood desk, swiveled toward each other, their steaming mugs on the little table between them.

For the next hour, they talked logistics and schedules and details. He was impressed by how much Gracie knew about ranching and the intelligent questions she asked. Granted, she'd been a hand for almost a decade, but she'd clearly been paying attention in a way some ranch hands didn't beyond the general scope of the job. She asked a lot of questions about their responsibilities as owners, and it was also clear that she'd done her homework and had read the materials the attorney had sent her.

He glanced at his phone on his knee. "Time to pick

up Alexa from her friend's house. Do you think we're set for today? You feel okay about your big start as co-owner of Heartland Hollows?"

"Definitely," she said. "I have a lot to learn, of course, but I feel comfortable. And I want you to know how much I appreciate the time you spent with me going over everything. Huge help."

"My pleasure. I'm always available, Gracie. Okay, off to get Alexa."

She smiled and sipped her coffee. "I remember my dad chauffeuring me around town to friends and outings and school events. And he used to walk me to the bus stop on weekday mornings and meet me in the afternoons just like you do. I begged him to stop when I was thirteen and started getting teased about being a baby."

"Oh, no doubt that's coming. She got a little mad at me this morning for insisting she wear a hat for the walk to the stop. It was freezing, though. Apparently, Lauren, one of her friends—announced at the lunch table recently that hats look stupid *and* mess up all their work on their hair before leaving for school."

Gracie sent him a compassionate smile. "There's a definite line between teaching a tween to follow her own instincts about what she thinks is right or stupid—and letting her find her way herself. That's what being twelve is about, right? Making decisions, whether right or wrong, and then either it feels good or it feels awful. Really cold ears is no fun but neither is feeling like a dork in a hat when everyone else isn't wearing one."

Huh. That was all very true. He'd been focused on the cold ears. "I guess I shouldn't have pushed the hat issue."

"Well, you get to have your say, too, West. It's hard to know when to let something go and when it matters. Yeah, if it's 10 degrees out, she should wear a hat for a quarter mile walk to the bus stop. But trust me, the minute she got on the bus, that hat came off and got shoved in her backpack. She won't get *off* the bus wearing it. I have a feeling if the issue drags on, it'll be you who backs down. Her ears, right?"

He stared at her in wonder. "You get it completely. I might be knocking on your door for advice every day."

She laughed. "Knock away. Honestly, West, I really admire how much you care about her feelings and tender psyche."

"Will I survive caring is the question," he said, standing up. He'd like nothing more than to get her advice about Alexa on a thousand other topics. But the way he found it hard to drag his eyes off Gracie, the way his nerve endings were all so fired up, had him kind of unsettled. "Well, off I go. Maybe she *will* come out with her favorite red wool ski hat—although, granted, it warmed up considerably this afternoon. I'll let you know."

She smiled, her pretty green eyes twinkling, and he was rooted in place. He didn't want to leave her company. He didn't want to stop looking at that face, stop hearing her voice.

Her phone rang and she eyed the screen. "Oh, good, it's Garland Jones—I'd emailed him with a few questions."

Just then, Liam, who'd been napping the past half hour, started fussing. Gracie popped up. She seemed to want to answer the phone *and* soothe the baby at the same time.

"You get the phone," he told her. "I'll get the baby."

She smiled with a look of relief as she grabbed her phone. Clearly, nothing she wanted to discuss with the lawyer was confidential for West's ears because she sat right back down and began talking to Jones. West plucked Liam from the bouncer and gave Gracie some privacy anyway, going through the open door to the living room.

"Hey, there, co-owner," West said as he rocked Liam in his arms while walking toward the sliding-glass doors to the deck. He gave his little back a few pats and a big burp came out—without any spit-up, West was glad to note, since he'd made the rookie move of not having a cloth. "Look, Liam, everything out there is ours. The snow lingering on the trees. That gorgeous red barn. The big green wreath. The fencing. I think your first word is gonna be *cow*."

Liam was staring at him, mesmerized by his big co-owner's face.

He was suddenly struck by a memory of standing by the sliding-glass doors in the foreman's cabin, holding Alexa, two and a half, in his arms, watching an early spring snow come down. Her mother gone just a few months then. Not a snowflake that tragic day or a slick road. Just a terrible accident. All his dreams for the three of them gone.

West sucked in a breath, willing himself to focus

on the baby he was holding. On the beautiful scene outside the windows.

Right now, this moment, was about a new beginning. He shut his eyes, forcing the old, painful thoughts to move back down deep, where he usually had a good lid on them. He opened his eyes to see his co-owner still staring at him, then a little fist reached out and grabbed the collar of his flannel shirt.

"Oh, so that's how it is," West whispered with a smile. *Babies can remind of you of so much, including how absolutely miraculous they are. Stay with that,* he told himself.

This *was* a fresh start. His second. The first was when he'd been hired as a cowboy at the Heartland Hollows ten years ago. A widower with a two-year-old.

Now he was an owner. With a twelve-year-old.

And this precious little guy in his arms.

And Gracie. A partner. A solely platonic partner.

Stay with the fresh start and don't let the past get a hold of you.

Or anything else.

Chapter Five

Gracie spent the next couple of hours in the ranch office, reading over her file on Heartland Hollows and going through the previous year's books. Between her meeting with West and this, she felt on solid ground with her understanding of how the ranch operated.

Where she was a little wobbly concerned how she felt around West himself. As a man. He was a little too easy on the eyes. His face and tall, strong body in those jeans—the way his broad shoulders filled out his flannel shirt.

The deadly combination of her unexpected physical attraction and how drawn to him as a person she was, was hard to shake off. What she'd thought would just be a harmless crush had scary potential to develop into something else. She *liked* West Calhoun. And she hadn't liked any man since her ex had deserted her after learning she was pregnant at seven weeks along.

Earlier this afternoon, when she'd ended her call with the attorney, West had been standing by the living room sliders, Liam in his arms, West telling him about the big green wreath that hung on the side of the barn. How it was tradition to hang it the first of December, how Bo Bixby had always loved Christmas, made an uncharacteristic fuss of decorating a tree between the main house and the working barns, giving a generous bonus to every employee and Christmas Eve and Christmas Day off. He'd also mentioned his arrangement with Alexa's grandparents that he'd have her birthdays and Christmas, and they could have all other holidays, spring break week and any weeks in summer they'd like. So, on Christmas, he made a small feast and always invited Bo. Some years he'd come, some he wouldn't.

He'd been telling Liam all this, and Gracie understood that West had forgotten where he was for the moment, that Gracie was in hearing distance in the office. West had been that lost in his thoughts, in his memories, speaking them out loud. Looking out at the vista did that to a person.

West Calhoun was grieving Bo's loss hard.

She'd waited in the doorway between the office and living room until he'd stopped talking. He was standing there by the window, just looking out, holding Liam so tenderly.

Her heart had squeezed in her chest. She'd given him a moment, then had come in. "You'll really feel his loss this Christmas," she'd said softly, and West had turned suddenly.

He'd seemed okay that she'd overheard. Glad, maybe. As if the fact that he was grieving, that this Christmas would be unusually hard, was out there, something he wouldn't have to explain if he was at all grinchy.

These moments—of not just getting to really know West but feeling close to him—were adding up.

And she was a little scared. She wasn't supposed to like West that way. And somehow she had to put the brakes on her brand-new feelings for a very good reason. Business partners had friction sometimes *without* the worry of a romance going sideways and creating big problems.

She had to be careful here to protect her son's future and legacy.

And herself. She might trust West Calhoun as a partner, but let another man anywhere near her heart when it had just begun to heal? No way.

The even scarier part was knowing that she had little control of how she felt. She had no idea what to do about that, so she decided to get busy, go see what needed doing in the barns.

With that settled, she now set Liam into his stroller in just his fleece jacket and hat since the barns were heated and she could easily unzip and remove the cap. As she approached the barns, Liam had already fallen asleep for his nap. Gracie could see a cowboy and cowgirl out in separate pastures. They were the only two on duty this afternoon, so she was sure she could help out in the barn, do some mucking and get her partner out of her head.

The barn was decently warm, so she parked Liam's stroller and unzipped his fleece and removed his hat, wondering if Alexa had come out of her friend's house with her own on or off. She smiled, her heart going out to West. A hat might seem like a small thing but there was so much to it, and a simple *Because I said so* could add a lot of resentment and tension to a household. Just like Alexa was figuring things out at twelve, so was West as a parent of a tween. The *sole* parent.

As Gracie gave Liam a kiss on the head and stood up straight, she thought she heard a voice. A whisper, really.

"Should I?" the voice said. A girl's voice.

Gracie listened, wondering if she'd imagined it.

"I mean, Penn is so cute," the girl whispered. "But he's kind of out of my league, right, Jackie?"

Hmm. Could that be Alexa talking to a friend somewhere in the barn?

Gracie moved across the aisle to the next row of stalls. Way down at the end, on the edge of a hay bale, she could see a jeans-clad leg and sneakered foot, green Converse, which an orange-and-white cat was rubbing her cheek against.

"I wish you could talk, Jackie," the girl continued in a whisper. "I need advice. And it's not like I can tell anyone about this. Not even Riley and Lauren. I mean, what if it gets around?"

Ah, Jackie was the cat. A true barn cat because, all of a sudden, the cat leapt off the hay bale and chased after something, then jumped back up beside the foot.

Gracie realized she'd better make her presence known before she overheard more than she should. "Hello?" she called out. "Thought I heard a voice."

Silence for a second, then feet landing on the ground.

A surprised girl peered around the hay bale. "Are you the other owner?"

"Yes," Gracie said with a smile, hurrying to get the stroller. She pushed it down the aisle where Alexa Calhoun was standing, the cat grooming herself on the hay bale. "I'm Gracie Dawson and this is my son, Liam. He's six months old. You must be Alexa."

She nodded. "And this is Jackie. She's my cat, but she likes to live in the barn, so we don't make her come inside our house."

"I can see why she likes this barn. Hay bales to jump on, things to chase after."

Alexa nodded. "I like it in here too. Sometimes, if I climb up in the hayloft no one even knows I'm here."

"Privacy," Gracie said. "I get it."

Alexa looked at Liam, who was still fast asleep. "Your baby is really cute." She was smiling and stepped closer, a bit shyly, then came close enough to peer down at Liam.

"Aww, thanks. He's a really good baby too." She smiled at the girl. "I should fess up. I heard you talking to Jackie when I first came in."

Alexa's cheeks flamed. She looked down—and unsure of herself. But then she said, "So you know I like someone."

"Penn is his name?" Gracie asked.

Alexa nodded and dropped down on the hay bale. "He's in two of my classes and sits right next to me in both, but I never know what to say so I never say anything."

"I know how that is," Gracie said, moving the stroller over so she could beside Alexa. "I did hear you tell the cat that you think he's out of your league. *No one* is out of your league."

Alexa tilted her head. "What do you mean? He's really popular. And really cute."

"Well, the way I see it, when two people like each other, nothing else matters except that. They like each other. Sometimes it's how someone makes you feel. Sometimes it's how easy it is to talk to them." *Your dad, for example*, she thought. "Sometimes you can't even explain it."

"I guess I see what you mean," Alexa said, tilting her head. "I never really thought of it that way." She seemed to brighten. "I do know why I like Penn. Because he's smart and not afraid to give an answer in class even when he might not be totally right. Like, if our English teacher asks a question about the book we're reading, he'll give an answer when sometimes I'm too afraid to. Sometimes it's even very close to what I'd say."

Gracie smiled.

"And he's *sooo* cute. He has brown eyes the color of a log, I think. And a ton of blond hair that's always in his eyes. I like how he shakes it away." She gave her head a *whoosh*, her own long hair flying, and Gracie laughed. Alexa did too.

"When I was in seventh grade, I had a huge crush on a boy who sounds a lot like Penn. His eyes were blue, though. I never even spoke to him once. I kept hoping he'd ask me to the seventh-grade holiday dance."

Alexa's eyes widened. This was definitely her kind

of conversation. "What happened? Did you ever talk to him? Did he ask you?"

"The first time we ever talked was because I asked him to the dance."

Alexa's mouth dropped open. "And what did he say?"

"He said he was going with his friends but when he got there, he'd find me and we'd dance, but only to a song he liked. Then he walked away. I was so disappointed at first. I thought he was just trying to let me down easy or something. But then he ran back and tapped me on the shoulder. I turned around and he said, 'If I don't like the song, I'll still dance with you.'" Gracie smiled at the memory. Tween puppy love. She could remember how clenched her stomach had been, how hopeful. All the worries and fears of first time emotions.

Alexa's eyes lit up. "That means he liked you too! And did you two dance?"

"Yup. In fact, he came and found me. He said, I love this song! Do you like it? And it was my favorite song at that time. We danced—for the next five songs in a row."

"And then you were like a couple?" she asked, hanging on Gracie's every word.

"Well, we probably would have been, but his mom's job got transferred out of state and they moved a week later!"

Alexa's mouth opened into an *O*. "That's so unfair!"

"Right? But I was so glad I was brave. It's all so hard."

"Tell me about it," Alexa said, biting her lip. "I'd never be able to ask Penn to even dance with me."

"Well, you could always try it if there's a dance coming up."

"There is, next Friday." She seemed to be thinking, then shook her head. "No way. I can't see asking him to dance. I can't even say hi."

Gracie smiled compassionately. She well remembered every bit of what this was like. A first crush. The fear. The hope. The nervous butterflies letting loose. Suddenly losing the ability speak or form thoughts.

"'Cuz if he liked me, he'd probably have talked to me by now," Alexa said. "He's not shy like I am."

"He might think the same way you do." Gracie added a sage nod.

"Maybe," she said, brightening again. "I can't wait for the dance. I'm going with my friends Riley and Lauren. We're best friends. We're all gonna wear the same purple dress, beaded bracelets with our names, and make our hair wavy. I tried watching videos on how to use the curling iron that my dad got me for Christmas last year, but every time I try wrapping my hair around the wand, it gets either stuck or slips out. My dad got me a whole set of hair stuff that I asked for, but I don't know what I'm doing."

Aww, of course West got her hair stuff. So sweet. Gracie could just picture him in the store, looking at all the boxes, maybe even asking a saleswoman for advice.

"I'd be happy to show you my tricks," Gracie said.

"I love adding beachy waves to my hair, which, as you can see, is stick straight."

"Could you show me?" Alexa asked, her eyes so hopeful.

Alexa was about to say a cheery *Sure* but then realized she should check in with West first before making...plans with his child. "We should definitely ask your dad about that first since it involves super-hot small appliances near your ears." She smiled to let Alexa know that was standard operating procedure when it came to someone else's kiddo.

But Alexa's face fell and she looked at the ground again. Then she knelt down and started petting the cat, not saying anything, eyes on Jackie. Gracie tried to figure out what might be making the girl uncomfortable about asking West's permission but wasn't coming up with anything.

"Did I hear something about hot appliances?" came a deep voice by the door.

Suddenly, Alexa shot up and ran off in the opposite direction. By the time West made his way over to where Gracie stood beside the stroller, she could see through the long horizontal windows that Alexa was racing toward the foreman's cabin across the gravel path. Huh. What was that about?

West followed Gracie's gaze and sighed. "Half the time I don't even know what I'm saying wrong. Small appliances?"

Gracie had such an urge to give West a hug. Wrap her arms around him and tell him this was par for the tween course, totally normal. And to try not to take it so personally, hard as that was when he cared so much, when he wanted a good relationship with his daughter, who was changing before his eyes. Twelve was *not* easy. But it wasn't hardest on the person going through it—for the first time. If Gracie had forgotten that, just talking to Alexa for the past five minutes—and her disappearing act—had made that *abundantly* clear.

Gracie wouldn't tell West that thirteen would come with its own new set of zingers. Fourteen and fifteen too. Luckily, sixteen was way off. No need to get into *that*.

But right now, the only thing she knew for sure she should do was keep her hands on the stroller to keep them *off* West Calhoun.

West still couldn't figure out the issue even after Gracie explained everything, from overhearing his daughter talking about her crush to the cat to Alexa asking if Gracie would show her how to give her hair "beachy waves."

It had taken a bit for him to get Gracie to tell him about the crush in the first place; she'd been resistant since it seemed private to her but he'd assured her he'd keep anything between the two of them. He just wanted to understand his daughter better.

"Why would asking me about using a curling iron make her upset—or uncomfortable?" West asked. He sat down on the hay bale, Gracie sitting beside him and giving the stroller a gentle roll. "I'm the one who bought her a hair kit with lots of different tools and styling products in the first place."

"I was trying to figure that out myself," she said, then an understanding came into her green eyes. "You know, I think I get it now. It's not about the curling iron. Or even the permission part. It's that you'll *know*."

"Know that she wants waves in her hair?"

"Know that she wants to try a new look—and *why*."

Ah. The lightbulb finally turned on over his head. "The crush. *Penn*." He inwardly sighed. Was he ready for that? No, he wasn't. He'd probably never be ready for all that.

She nodded. "Exactly. And it appears to be her first one—first real one."

He mock shivered. "Twelve is the age, right? When it all starts. Boys, makeup, clothes, the mall, friends whispering in groups. And, oh, God—wondering about kissing."

"Yup."

He dropped his head back and stared up at the barn ceiling, but Jackie the cat chose that moment to jump right on his lap. She was all of eight, nine pounds, but that was quite an unexpected thud.

Gracie laughed and petted the orange-and-white tabby along her back.

"It was nice of you to offer your help," he said. "Thank you. And I mean that, but I'm saying it right now because I'm at a loss. As to how to navigate this. Of course she doesn't want to talk crushes with me. Particularly her first crush. She's stuck with a dad as her only parent. No cool aunt either. Her maternal grandmother is great, but I can't see Alexa reaching out to her with this kind of thing."

"Well, then I guess it's gonna be the two of you, figuring it out as you go along. It's why they say necessity is the mother of invention."

"I guess so," he said with a smile.

Gracie smiled, too, and the way her pretty face lit up made it very hard to glance away. "All I know for sure is that I'm really glad you're here right now. You're very easy to talk to, Gracie Dawson. I might have said that already."

"Or I did about you."

He gave her hand a squeeze because he was just so...happy she was sitting next to him, gently guiding him along this unfamiliar territory.

Maybe just the way you are with her and the ranch, he thought suddenly. Huh. Maybe so.

"And go right ahead," he added. "Helping Alexa with her waves, I mean."

Gracie looked so happy. "Great. Tell her to knock on the door anytime she wants to practice before the dance."

She gave his arm a pat, and even over his shirtsleeve, he *felt* that touch. Even when she moved her hand back to the stroller, that area on his forearm tingled. That he was attracted to this woman, on a few levels, was undeniable. Surprising for him, but undeniable.

"I should be prepared for all that, right? I've been her dad for the past twelve years. Every year has brought something new. And then there are times when I'm in town or I'm picking up Alexa from a friend's house, I see dads who seem so at ease with their tweens."

"They're probably thinking the same about you," she said. "Everyone's in the same boat with slightly different choppy waters."

He nodded, taking that in. She was right. "I always think that no matter what her attitude and tone says, she actually needs *more* of me, not less. But she's changing so fast before my eyes that it makes my head spin. Her first crush on a boy. Caring about clothes and her hair when she never did before. Hating that she supposedly smells like cow, which she said the other day at breakfast when she smelled like clean soap and strawberry shampoo."

Gracie smiled and was about to give Jackie a scratch on her neck when she leapt down. "I think you're right about that, West. That Alexa does need more of you, not less. She might not always appreciate that, but less is not more when it comes to being there for your twelve-year-old daughter."

"Okay, good that you think so. Because it's what my instincts tell me. But then, just when I think we're okay, that we're getting back that closeness, she retreats again. I never know if I should give her space and privacy or if I should check in."

He found himself telling her about what happened when he'd met Alexa's bus yesterday, the conversation about being new co-owners and how she—Gracie—seemed to him like a loving, doting mother. How Alexa had run off and gone into the cave he'd built for her in her room. Her safe place.

"She was okay almost right away, but it's another example of how I want to get fatherhood right. Was I supposed to stay longer with her in her room and talk more about her mom? Or let her have some privacy with her feelings?"

"Oh, West," Gracie said, and the compassion in her expression went straight into his heart. "You're doing everything right. Of course you are. By wondering about *any* of this in the first place. The way I see it, and take this with a grain of salt since I'm not her parent, is that there are really just two things you need to know when it comes to talking to your daughter. One is to *never* ignore how she feels—which includes dismissing and inadvertently mocking. The other is not to smother her—by projecting or using yourself as a guide for how she *should* feel."

He tilted his head. "Uh, what's in between those two? Because there's where I'd like to be."

She smiled gently. "That's exactly where you are. It's why you don't have to worry so much about how you're doing. That's what I meant by you're doing everything right."

He sat with that for a second. "You actually made me feel better. *A lot* better. I just don't want to screw this up. I don't even have my own experience to use as a guide."

Now she tilted her head. "What do you mean?"

"My father died when I was a baby. My mom never remarried. She always said no other man would ever measure up. And she once added that she was worried she'd end up with someone who wouldn't be the father I deserved. I think she was just heartbroken."

"You've been single for ten years," she said softly.

Was she wondering if he felt the same? That no one would measure up to his late wife?

He thought about that. Hard.

He'd loved Jenny so much. And for those early years, especially when their daughter was so little, that may have been true. That no one could be a mama for Alexa like Jenny would have been—had she had the opportunity, the damned luck.

But for the past five years, he'd say, he'd been ready to find someone he knew would have that special seal of approval—his own list of what was important for himself and Alexa. He just hadn't found her. Maybe one day he'd explain all this to Gracie, but now, when he barely knew her, was not the right time.

"Not for lack of trying not to be," he said. "You know what dating is like. I've been wondering lately if I should use the 'two out of three ain't bad' approach. Maybe I'm asking for too much in all three—to be in love, to share the same values, outlook, hopes for the future, and most importantly, that she be an excellent stepmother to Alexa."

"Um, which would this potential love interest give up? I'd say it has to be the first, since the second and third are reliant on each other to coexist."

"Yeah, I guess so since we'd need to be on the same page, particularly when it came to parenting and raising Alexa together through her teen years."

"So you'd give up being in love? To be so overwhelmed by your feelings for someone that you know they're the one?"

Would he? Maybe he had already gone in that direction without realizing it. Maybe he was only looking for the excellent stepmother.

"Maybe?" he asked. "I need to focus on other things, not being crazy in love."

She was quiet for a moment. "I'm a single parent, too, so I get it. It just feels…wrong somehow. Honestly, I'm not sure I even believe in it anymore, though. Falling madly in love and all that—it doesn't last. True love, does, though. Like my parents have. Like my grandparents had when my grandpa was alive. Based on a *real* relationship, not lust and a honeymoon period." She bit her lip and turned away.

The cat jumped up between them again just then, a welcome interloper. She put a paw on Gracie's thigh and then just jumped right on her lap and curled up.

"Jackie is a great judge of character," he said, scratching the cat behind her ears. This conversation had started out hard and now it was even harder. How on earth had they gotten here? Talking about real love? What they believed in and didn't?

She looked at him so suddenly that their lips were just inches apart. It would be so easy to just lean in a bit. To give in to the deep urge he felt. The deep interest.

Don't do it, he told himself. *The two of you have a nice working relationship right now. Don't do anything to mess that up. You'll be in partnership with*

Gracie for twenty years. A kiss lasts fifteen seconds. Sex—an hour, maybe.

That was what she'd been talking about. Lust. Honeymoon period.

And how fleeting it all was.

He hated how cynical he'd become about relationships. But if nothing had worked out for those ten years Gracie had noted, why would this? And if he had every reason to protect his partnership with her—and her baby son by default—then he'd do exactly that. Protect it.

He leaned back a bit. Out of kissing distance.

"I really appreciate the hair help," he said fast, shifting another inch away. "If Alexa brings up anything to do with her looks and I make the slightest comment, she shuts that down immediately. You've got her seal of approval in five seconds."

Gracie smiled. "I'm happy to help. I'm an only, like you, so no nieces to fuss over. I'm home nights any time she wants to come by."

"I have no doubt she will want to. Thanks, Gracie. Really," he added, happy for his daughter.

It was himself he was worried about.

Chapter Six

The moment Gracie was back in the house after that unexpected encounter with both Alexa and West, she video-called her best friend. The familiarity of Miranda's face, her words of wisdom, and insightful outlook never failed to buoy Gracie when she was feeling unsure or out of her element. Like now. She'd had a warm welcome to the Heartland Hollows, and she might know the basics of how ranches worked, but she had a lot to learn. That she felt unmoored had as much to do with West and her attraction to him than the sudden inheritance and new home.

And *she* was giving him parent advice? She had a *baby*.

Gracie wished she could send a quick text suggesting she and Miranda meet for coffee in a half hour and split something big and decadent, but Miranda was away and would be the entire month of December. Her painful divorce had been finalized just a few months ago, and she'd treated herself to a long-time dream of attending a yoga teaching training retreat seven hours away in Jackson Hole. Just two weeks into the program, Gracie could see a peaceful strength in her friend's expression.

Now, they caught each other up on their lives, Miranda actually gasping at everything that was going on with Gracie back home in Bear Ridge.

"Wow," Miranda said. "Wow."

"Right?"

"I'm dying to hear more about West Calhoun," Miranda said with a twinkle in her pretty hazel eyes. "But I've got a burning question first. Why did this Bo Bixby dude leave half his ranch to a *baby* if they're not related?"

"Right? *Why?*" There was a lot going on at Heartland Hollows, but the mystery of this was never far from Gracie's thoughts.

"Let's go through every possible scenario for why a total stranger left your baby son, who he'd never met, half his zillion-dollar ranch. Bixby also knew Liam's *birthday*, where he was born, and *your* name."

Gracie flopped down on the sofa and curled her legs up to her chest. The baby in question was still napping in his stroller, and Gracie had him parked beside the coffee table with a view of his mama in case he quietly woke up and she was too busy gabbing to notice. "I've run through every possibility I can think of and have come up blank."

"Okay, like what? Let's dissect."

Worth a try. Gracie had done this with her parents and grandmother and nothing anyone had said made them go, *Aha, that must be it!*

Miranda picked up a glass containing some kind of

green juice and took a sip. "Since you can't find the connection between yourself and Bo Bixby, then it *has* to be between Bo and Liam's father."

Gracie froze for a second. Huh. "That's a good way to look at it. I definitely didn't know Bo, never met him, and my parents and grandmother haven't either. My mom knew his name from when he first moved to Bear Ridge ten years ago. Apparently, all the single ladies had had their eye on him. But it seems like, if he dated a lot, it was 'never with the same woman twice' kind of thing. He never married, never had kids."

"That anyone is aware of," Miranda said.

Again, Gracie froze. The thought hadn't occurred to her. "But Bo apparently wasn't aware he had a child either. The last ten years, anyway. And if Harry was his secret son or something like that, how would Bo have known about me at all? And Liam's birth?"

"Yeah, no clue. We're missing something, definitely. Okay, let's drop the family angle for a minute. You're sure Harry didn't work for Bo at some point? A favorite ranch hand or something?"

"West has been at Heartland Hollows for the past ten years, which is how long Bo has owned the place, and he's never heard of Harry."

"Hmm," Miranda said, tapping her chin. "Could they have known each other prior? Like wherever Bo lived before, Harry was a big part of his life or did him some huge favor?"

"I guess it's possible, but then ten years go by with Harry not making an appearance at Heartland Hollows? How big a part of his life could Harry have been?"

"Big enough to know that Harry had a baby, and on what day, and the mother's name."

Right. Gracie was plain stumped. "It just doesn't make sense. West said that Bo had no family. I don't know anything about his parents or grandparents or relatives. But no family is no family—unless there were estrangements."

She tried to imagine being estranged from any of her relatives. The thought alone was unbearable.

"You just never know what someone's story is," Miranda said. "Why this or that. You said Bo and West were close, but it sounds like West doesn't know anything about the man either."

"I know. I think West felt close to him—but not because Bo was forthcoming about his life story or anything to do with him personally. I guess it was more a ranch thing, mentee and mentor. I know West is grieving the loss hard."

Miranda was taking all that in. "So if Bo didn't talk about his life, maybe there are secrets that West just doesn't know anything about. Maybe Harry was Bo's long-lost son? A kid he never knew about until right before he died? Or maybe he knew he had a son and they were estranged?"

"I mean, it's possible. But it seems so unlikely. No contact in the ten years since West had been at the ranch? Or when Bo was dying of cancer? If Harry was his son and that meant enough to Bo to leave

Harry's baby half the ranch, why wouldn't Bo have reached out?"

"Well, you did just say that Bo didn't even talk about his personal life with the one person *in* his life. Bo sounds like a very private person."

Gracie frowned. "I guess. It's just all so hard to fathom. Being so alone in the world—if you weren't. If you did have family—and a child? An adult son?"

"Okay, let's stay with that. Harry died in the motorcycle accident just a few months after Liam was born. If Harry and Bo were related but had no contact, how *would* Bo have found out anything about Liam's birth?"

"Exactly my question," Gracie said. "Harry hadn't cared about his son being born to the point that he didn't call me or stop by to even ask a single question about his child—" She paused. Gracie *hated* remembering that. She let out a sigh. "Yet Harry made a point of sharing information about his newborn, his birthday and the name of his mother with his long-lost father?" She shook her head. "I don't get it. We have to be barking up the wrong tree, as they say."

Miranda nodded. "Yeah, that they're related, particularly father and long-lost son, does seem farfetched. And if Harry had simply been a cowboy on Bo's ranch wherever he lived before, what kind of impact could an eighteen-year-old kid make on a ranch owner to the point he'd leave his baby half his ranch?"

"All this makes me want to cross the Harry connection off the list of possibilities. But it's the best possible link. That's the problem. Because nothing about it adds up."

"We're missing something. Maybe even something obvious. There's a piece of information you and West just don't have, Gracie."

"Exactly. But where are we going to get it from if Bo has no family or friends? His lawyer said they were old friends, but West said he never saw the two together in the ten years West was at Heartland Hollows. And the lawyer didn't know the name Harry Ahern. I asked."

"Back to square one," Miranda said. "Okay, let's say *you're* the connection to Bo. Think of every time in the past…say, five years, that you did a stranger a good deed or big favor. That stranger *was* Bo Bixby and remembered you. He had no family, so he left you half his ranch."

"Left *Liam* half his ranch. If I'd been the one who'd meant something special, he would have left it to *me*."

"Oh, right. Ahhh," Miranda said, faux-grabbing fistfuls of her long brown hair. "This is giving me a headache," she added on a laugh. She took another sip of her green juice. "Spinach, kale with a splash of almond milk," she said holding it up and taking a gulp.

"I'll stick with eggnog since I'm not contorting my body into various hard poses for long seconds." At six months after giving birth, Gracie's body wasn't quite back to the "before." Nothing about her post-baby soft body bothered her. It all gave her Liam.

Miranda laughed. "I only have a few minutes left before meditation class. So, on to my other burning question. Do you think something will happen between you and West?"

She suddenly imagined her and West in a steamy kiss. Mouths fused. Hands roaming. Chest to chest. The anticipation of more...

She felt that in all her nerve endings.

"I admit—despite my trust level being at an all-time low, I'm *so* attracted to him. He's very easy to look at and talk to. But something *can't* happen, right? That's just a bad idea. Too much can go wrong. We're business partners. Can you imagine if we hate each other's guts over a romantic relationship gone south? It'll ruin everything."

No kiss was worth that.

And she'd hardly want to stop at a kiss.

"Who says the relationship would end, let alone badly?" Miranda said with a devilish twinkle. "Do you believe *I'm* saying that? Me? I'm telling you, Gracie—just two weeks at this yoga retreat, all the meditating and silent sessions, eating so healthily and staring at the stars and snowcapped trees, and I feel a lot more positive about everything, including my romantic future. Not every guy will be my ex. Or yours. West Calhoun could be as forever as the Heartland Hollows Ranch."

Except nothing is forever.

Maybe Gracie should take up yoga. Be more positive.

Who was she kidding? She had too much to protect for that. Including herself.

And anyway, West seemed to be looking for something very specific in a partner for himself. And his checklist didn't necessarily include being in love. He'd have to care deeply for her, she was sure. Like her very much. But he'd forego being in love if it meant she'd make a great life partner, a great stepmother.

He was taking the sensible approach, and she didn't begrudge him that. She just wished it were possible to have it all. And maybe it wasn't. Maybe you did have to give up some old dreams to have new ones. Or to fit the *you* you were now.

But at least Miranda was in a very good place at the moment where the heart was concerned. Bouncing back, coming around again.

"I love that, Miranda. You deserve all the happiness in the world. I guess I'm at yellow for caution."

"Nothing wrong with that." Miranda seemed about to add something then thought better of it because she said, "I'd better get going. Oh, and if you wake up in the middle of the night with a possible idea for how Liam is connected to Bo, call me. Same if you and West end up in bed."

Gracie smiled. "Trust me, I definitely will. Miss you, Mir."

"Me too. But I'll be back right after New Year's and we'll have a lot to celebrate. A new me and a brand-new life for you just when you needed it."

Huh. Gracie supposed she had needed something—something to get her out of the grind of just getting by, working so hard to pay her bills and not being able to save, wanting more for Liam and twisting herself in knots over not having something to leave him, like a savings account let alone a house. She had three hundred and sixty-one dollars in a college fund for him. And she'd opened that, determined to transfer twenty-five dollars a month from her paycheck, the day after she'd told Harry Ahern about the pregnancy. The day after she'd known she was on her own. Not even four hundred bucks in a little over a year.

Her parents had told her she'd always been too hard on herself, that she was doing great, and that as a single mom whose baby's father walked out on her without a penny in child support, she should be focused on how strong she was, not what she was supposedly lacking.

She appreciated that. So much. But this security—Heartland Hollows, the inheritance—had changed her life completely.

"I'm just saying, keep an open mind," Miranda said. "Because from what you told me about West, he sounds *amazing*. Okay, gotta run—love you. Bye!"

Just as she ended the video call, her phone pinged with a text.

West. As if talking about him had conjured him right up.

Is now a good time for Alexa to come over? I told her you said it was a hair thing you two had been talking about in the barn and that it was fine with me if she wanted your help, and her whole face lit up.

Aww.
She texted back.

You handled that just right—no mention of the crush!

Hey, I'm not THAT out of touch.

He added an emoji of a smiley face in sunglasses.

She'll be over in thirty. And thank you.

Her heart was doing a little too much fluttering. She really did like this man.
She sent back a smiley face of her own.
But ending up in bed like Miranda had mentioned—not going to happen. *Could not* happen.

A hour and a half after those texts between him and Gracie, West was walking over to the ranch house to pick up Alexa since it got dark early now. He felt so lucky that Gracie Dawson had dropped into his life out of the clear blue—and in such a big way. That his new co-owner of Heartland Hollows should turn out to be someone his daughter could turn to…how on earth had he gotten so lucky?

Right now, this woman he hadn't known last week was helping his daughter style her hair, and very likely, they were chatting away about the dance and all it engendered for Alexa. Like her crush. Topics Alexa wouldn't have raised with him. Yes, he felt lucky. And grateful.

And once again, he'd opened up to her. He thought about all he and Gracie had talked about in the barn. What he was looking for in a woman he'd settle down with. How stepmother material had become the most important thing and being madly in love had fallen by the wayside. Or just didn't seem to matter the way it once had.

He was thirty-six years old with a twelve-year-old daughter. Of course his feelings on that had changed. Or evolved.

Didn't matter. He wasn't getting involved with anyone in the immediate future, particularly Gracie. He'd already deemed himself lucky. He was not going to *push* that luck.

His phone vibrated in his pocket and a glance at the screen showed his friend Breyer's name.

He and Breyer had grown up together in Bear Ridge, but the guy had had wanderlust and wanted to see the entire USA, state by state. From a ranching family, too, Breyer had gotten jobs as a cowboy and a hand at all kinds of ranches across the country. Now married with a five-year-old daughter, he'd put down roots at a dairy farm in Maine, where his wife was originally from, since his folks were both gone. West was determined to get there for a visit someday. According to Breyer, Wyoming got a hell of a lot colder in winter than Maine did, so maybe he'd wait until a warm spring.

"It's been like a month since we last talked," Breyer said. "Catch me up. How's my favorite preteen? *How* is she twelve already?"

Oh, man. A lot had happened in that month. In the past *week*. Despite how close he and his buddy had always been, sometimes even a few months would pass between calls. Breyer was super busy as a husband, dad, and running his farm, and it was the same for West minus the wife.

"Alexa's doing great. She's on the track team and will try out for cross-country in the spring. She has her besties, which I know is vital for this age. She probably wishes *I* had more of a clue, though."

Breyer laughed. "Forewarned for seven years from now."

West pictured his friend's adorable five-year-old, Bella, with her curly, white-blond hair. Her favorite color was orange and unless she was wearing it in some capacity, she refused to leave the house. He smiled at the thought. And got very nostalgic for Alexa as a little girl.

"In fact, you'll never guess where Alexa is at the moment." West glanced around to make sure no one was in hearing distance. He was still far enough from the house that his voice wouldn't carry to a possibly open window or to the ears of Gracie and Alexa sitting on the porch in their jackets, enjoying hot cocoa on a not-freezing evening. Then he told Breyer everything, including the part about six-month-old Liam Dawson inheriting half Heartland Hollows, and swore his friend to secrecy on that since he and Gracie wanted to keep it quiet until they figured out the mystery.

"If I'm dead quiet," Breyer said, "it's because I'm both absorbing everything you just told me and trying to process it. Wow, West."

"Yup," he agreed. Wow. All around.

"You know me," Breyer added. "I'll go poke around

in the barn and call you back—maybe tonight, maybe next week, maybe in a year—with my theories on how that baby is linked to your late boss. Right now, every time something comes to mind, I dismiss it."

"Yeah, Gracie and I have done a lot of that."

"'Gracie and I,'" Breyer said. "Has a ring to it."

West could hear the smile in his friend's voice. "Speaking of that, I need you to confirm something for me so I have your voice *and* mine in agreement in my head on the subject. It involves Gracie and these very…unexpected feelings I'm having. I like her a little too much—on every level. But we're co-owners. Partners. I screw that up in any way and it's the next generation who suffers. We have to be careful, right?"

"West, who on planet earth is more cautious than you are? Have more faith in yourself. If you like this woman—if she's helping your daughter with her hair, for God's sake—it's because you have a degree of trust in her."

Yeah but. That was problem. That he did have that trust. That he did have feelings. They had to stay platonic for reasons that had nothing to do with him or her and everything to do with the ranch—protecting the ranch.

"Look, I'm sure there are some complications," Breyer said. "When aren't there, for whatever reason? But I like where this is heading. And I like the sounds of Gracie. Strong feelings for a woman—*good* thing. Being cautious—to a *point*—also a good thing. Just go with it, West."

Just go with it. He didn't know about that. Being able to do that.

He reminded Breyer that Gracie was his *business partner*—for the next twenty years until her baby son came of age to take over management of his half of the ranch. That there was that very old, very famous, saying about not mixing business and pleasure for a *reason*. "You know, you might remember Gracie from school since you two were closer in age than I am with you guys." West was seven years older than Gracie. And he had five years on his friend.

"Honestly, there were so many Dawsons in Bear Ridge that I could never keep them straight," Breyer said. "I hear what you're saying about how a breakup—a bad breakup—could interfere with you two running the ranch. But if you think that'll keep you two from getting together..." He gave an evil mwah-ha-ha laugh.

"Even though a bad ending puts the ranch in jeopardy?"

"Who says you'll have a bad ending? But, for the sake of argument, let's say you do. Let's say you hook up or get seriously involved and things fall apart and you break up. You're both hurt and pissed at each other. I don't see you letting that affect the ranch. You're you, West. Careful, pragmatic, focused. You'll put the ranch first before your scorched heart or whatever."

Huh. That did sound like him. He'd put the ranch first. He knew it.

"If you feel something for this woman, and it's clear you do, then go with it, West. You've been unable to commit to anyone all these years because you hadn't found her yet. Maybe now you have. Between the strong feelings and her being stepmother material, you just might have found what you've always been looking for."

He froze for a second. Breyer was getting way ahead of himself. "We barely know each other."

"Sorry, buddy, but something's happening beyond your control. Hers, too, I'm sure. There's too much at stake to let stupid issues, whatever might crop up, derail the romance. You'll work things through because you *need* to. Walking away won't be easy, like it is for most couples who don't have legal documents in their way. In fact it'll be impossible. You'll *have* to figure things out."

Huh. "That's a good point." He'd think about that.

West was approaching the house. He could see Alexa and Gracie's silhouettes in an upstairs window.

"Uh-oh, West, I've gotta go. The Chihuahua knocked into Bella's Lego tower and she's sobbing. Let me know what happens. And one more thing…"

"What's that?" West asked.

"I'm really happy for you. I've been waiting to hear that some great woman managed to get under the lock and key."

West smiled. "You're getting way ahead of yourself again."

"Famous last words," Breyer said, then disconnected.

There was a good reason West's heart was under that lock and key. Loss was extremely painful, and hard, and took a long time to deal with. He had a twelve-year-old daughter who needed him more than she knew or wanted. And West would not let her down. And he had a ranch to protect. His and Alexa's future, Alexa's legacy. All very good reason to be practical.

He headed up the porch steps and rang the doorbell. A few seconds later, he could hear footsteps approaching from inside, a little thud on the floor, likely Alexa's backpack containing her hair kit and everything else she'd packed for the visit here.

It was Alexa who opened the door with a shy smile, Gracie behind her.

West froze and stared at his daughter—who didn't look like his daughter.

She looked like...a teenager.

Like his beloved, wonderful, sweet, smart Alexa Joy Calhoun—wearing shimmery shadow on her eyelids, a little mascara, he was pretty sure, sparkly purple lip gloss, her hair in waves down past her shoulders. And instead of the brightly colored nail polish she sometimes wore, alternating colors every nail, her nails were also a dark purple.

Which matched the dress she'd bought on a shopping trip with her friends to Brewer.

He wasn't quite sure what his expression was saying but it was enough to make Alexa's excited, happy face fall.

Before he could say a word, before he could do anything, she took off running toward the foreman's cabin.

Oh, no. Dammit.

"West, I—" Gracie started to say, her expression a mix. Worry. Disappointment.

"I'll go after her," he said, and unexpectedly couldn't form more words.

Gracie nodded and suddenly things were awkward—for the first time since that first half hour in the lawyer's office. "West, you might not be ready for the girl who opened the door. But she *is* that girl. It's not what's next. It's what right now. Appropriately so."

He hurriedly clasped her hand in acknowledgment, in thanks, not that he'd shown *any* appreciation. Dammit again. He grabbed the backpack and rushed out after his Alexa, slinging it over his shoulder.

The path between the house and their cabin was illuminated and safe, but it *was* dark and cold and, thanks to him and his stupid reaction, Alexa had run it alone, likely crying.

He'd screwed up with the one thing he was so desperate to get right: his relationship with his daughter.

Gracie had been one hundred percent right. He might not be ready for this, for the girl who'd appeared in that doorway looking so grown up, for everything that represented and would mean.

But Alexa was ready.

And he had to do a better job of handling all the changes she was going through at twelve—and that he was going through as her dad.

Her sole parent.

He hadn't felt this unmoored with his daughter since the night he'd lost his wife, her mother.

How West wished there were a manual, chapters in black and white. *This is going to happen and when it does, do this, say that.* Which was ridiculous. People were individuals. No two would go through the exact same thing the exact same way.

And no one wanted a parent who gave stock answers about life.

Go fix this, he told himself, and went into the cabin, everything suddenly upside down.

Chapter Seven

West headed upstairs, sure he'd find Alexa in her room, in one of the nooks and crannies he'd built for her. But as he walked down the hall toward her door, he could see she was in the bathroom, standing in front of the vanity, staring at herself in the mirror. Not frowning. Not smiling.

When she heard him coming, she turned, her back to the door, then stepped into the tub and sat down on the rim, facing the shower wall. Away from him.

"Lex, I want to first say that I think you look great. Beautiful. Your makeup and hair and nails and—"

"You obviously thought I look stupid," she said, looking down. "I could see it in your face. If you'd thought I looked good, you would have said so."

He took a chance of sitting beside her on the bathtub rim. She didn't move over, so that was a good sign. "When I first saw you, wearing makeup and your hair in waves, my immediate reaction was, Where did my baby girl go? How is she twelve? Where is that five-, eight-, ten-year-old? How is Alexa almost a teenager?"

He glanced at her, relieved to see her expression had softened.

"You know that picture of us on my bedside table," he continued, "the one where you're just a baby, four months old, in that pink snowsuit? Every night when I go to bed, every morning when I wake up, I see that photo of you. But babies grow up and it gets parents emotional. When I saw you wearing makeup for the first time, your hair done differently than usual, I got hit with all those feelings. How you're not that baby anymore. You're moving into a whole new phase. Dances. Hair. Nails that match your dress."

She turned slightly toward him. She was biting her lip, but he could see confidence coming back into her face. "I really like my dress. Riley and Lauren and I all have the same one, but different colors. Their nails will match too. We're all going to have waves in our hair."

This is who she is now, coming into her own, needing to feel like one of the group. Let her be, let her discover who she is her way.

"Your hair looks great, Alexa," he said with a nod. He touched where the wave dipped in. "You look great. Absolutely beautiful."

He could see the smile spreading on her face, and she knocked her knees into him.

Now he smiled, finally.

She looked at him. "Gracie taught me how to use the curling iron and also gel and hair spray. She's so nice. I'm so happy she's the co-owner."

"Me too."

Alexa turned and slid her feet over the rim to the floor. She got up and moved to the vanity, standing in front of the big mirror. He swiveled around but stayed put. "Even though I'm wearing makeup and my hair's done, I'm still the same inside, Dad."

His heart pinged. He stood and moved next to her, putting an arm around her shoulder. "I really appreciate that you said that. Because you'll always be my baby, my little girl. No matter how old you are."

She made a face, then laughed. "Oh, I forgot to ask before, Riley's hosting a study party tomorrow night for our American history unit test. I can go, right? Her parents are ordering in pizza and making cupcakes. It's from four to eight."

"Sounds great," he said.

She beamed and dashed off for her room.

He sucked in a breath, then went into his bedroom and shut the door. He took out his phone and called Gracie. The sound of her voice saying hi on the other end was a balm.

"I talked to Alexa," he said. "We're okay. *She's* okay. I basically told her my nostalgia for my baby girl got the better of me, but that I think she looks great—beautiful."

"Aww, West, I can understand that."

"She told me that makeup or not, she's still the same inside." He shook his head in wonder. "My child is smarter than me. I have to deal with that now too."

Gracie laughed. "You two will be just fine. I have no doubt."

"I appreciate that. I also appreciate that you helped her with her dance look. Even if I'm not ready for it."

"My pleasure, really. She's a great girl."

An idea hit him, and he told himself to keep it to

himself, to quash it. To forget it. But that lasted for two seconds.

He wanted to make the very pleasant thought in his head a reality—and that was that.

"I just found out I'm on my own for dinner tomorrow night, so if you and Liam are free, I could come bearing the makings for my specialty—spaghetti and meatballs—as a thank-you for tonight—for all of it. Being there for her in the barn. Helping her with her look. Dealing with me being *that* dad."

He paused. This sounded like a date. A thank-you would involve a ten-dollar gift card to Bear Ridge Coffee. *No, not a date*, he told himself. *A date is a thing, formal. This is just a casual at-home dinner for reasons—a thanks.* That had him feeling better about it.

But he wanted to be in Gracie's company again. Not just in passing on the ranch either.

He rushed to add, "And I could answer any Heartland Hollows questions you might have now that it's been a couple days."

"I actually have a list of questions I've been keeping in the notes app on my phone. That sounds great, West. And Liam will try his very first taste of a meatball. If he takes after his mama, he'll be in heaven. I have Italian bread to contribute to the meal."

"We're all set then," he said. "I'll need to pick up Alexa at eight from her friend's study party, so how about I come over at five thirty? It's on the early side, but since it's a working dinner..."

There it was. A working dinner. Not a date.

"Five thirty is great—"

He could hear Liam let out a sharp cry in the distance. "I'll let you go. See you tomorrow."

They disconnected and for a good fifteen seconds he held on to the phone, wondering what he'd just gotten himself into.

The next night, Gracie had just settled Liam into his high chair in the kitchen when the doorbell rang.

West. She was a little too excited about their plans. Last night, as she'd gotten into bed, she'd thought about his call and how close to him she felt. He was opening his life to her, whether he'd expected to or not, and she'd bank on not.

She hadn't been able to stop thinking of him. Imagining him in bed, too, maybe bare-chested and wearing only sweatpants. And possibly thinking about her as well.

She liked the idea of having him to herself in this capacity—cooking together, eating together. Tonight felt almost like a date.

But in the five seconds it took to get to the door, she was reminded that getting involved with West—if that was where a night like tonight was headed—was complicated. They needed to have a good, solid partnership. And what romantic relationship had Gracie ever had that hadn't ended either in disappointment and hurt feelings or with total heartbreak. She'd never been one to casually date, so her heart had always been fully in from the start. There was definitely something between her and West. Add her attraction to him—

on all levels—and she'd find it very difficult to turn off her feelings to stick to the necessary friendship.

Before you open that door and see his gorgeous face, you should get something straight with yourself. You should remember that this is about Liam's legacy and future, and protecting what's his.

Well, that did make it a lot easier. This wasn't and couldn't be a date. Period.

And then she opened the door. Dammit. What was so irresistible was how kind and thoughtful and full of integrity he was. The face and body combined with all that...deadly.

Who says that a new relationship with a man of integrity will lead to disappointment and heartbreak— and set the partnership on a bad course? Why not have faith that if you let something sweet and beautiful happen, it could lead to happiness?

Because it had never happened before, that's why.

She sighed.

"I brought everything we need for dinner," he said with a smile, holding up his grocery bag.

As she led the way into the large kitchen, she was so aware of him next to her that the space felt tiny.

He set the bag on the counter and turned to Liam. "Hey, there, little guy. How are you today? You get to try the best meatball of your life. Yeah, yeah, you're only six months old and it'll be your first, but today's meatball will never be topped."

Gracie laughed. "You're pretty confident."

"Because he *is* only six months and it *is* his first meatball."

She grinned and gave his arm a little squeeze before she could stop herself. *No need to touch him, Gracie. Those little, supposedly casual touches are what lets someone know you're interested*—that way.

Especially because he looked at her just then and it was very clear that he'd *felt* that touch. Goose bumps broke out along her spine, up her arms.

That there was something between them had never been the issue. There was.

"Buh-ya!" Liam said, waving his hand around with a big grin of his own.

Thank you, Liam, for defusing the moment, for giving me somewhere to look besides West Calhoun's handsome face and hot body.

He looked particularly sexy tonight for no reason at all. He wore a navy Henley shirt, the three buttons unbuttoned. Jeans. He wore wool socks, variegated browns. No jewelry. His thick, dark hair was its usual tousled. The slightest of five-o'clock shadow. Her gaze kept dropping to his lips.

Then to the sexy crinkles at the corners of his eyes as he turned to her. "Liam is saying 'Well, get on with it, bud. Make me this supposedly great ball of meat.'"

Gracie laughed again. "Okay then. Let's hop to it."

For the next ten minutes, they set up and laid out. West suggested cooking the meatballs in sauce so they'd stay soft for Liam, and there went her heart. A man who made the most basic of decisions—whether to fry, bake or let the meatballs cook in sauce in a pot—based on her baby son's needs…that was a man to take a risk for.

There it was. What her heart had been saying lately. What Miranda had been trying to tell her.

He was a man to take a risk for.

"I'll have you know that Alexa insisted on no hat today because her hair was still wavy and she wanted to show her friends. I didn't a say a word."

Gracie smiled. "And you probably were relieved that it wasn't crazy cold at just before 8:00 a.m."

"True." He turned to her, the package of ground beef in his hand. "Listen. I just want to say again—thank you. For everything yesterday. You were there multiple times in multiple ways—each great. And each time you told me what I needed to hear."

She could feel a blush rise to her cheeks—that was how pleased she was by what he'd said. "My pleasure, really."

"I kept thinking yesterday, How did I get so lucky that you turned out to be the co-owner? Well, Liam. I could have ended up with some awful grumpy jerk—and instead I got the two of you."

Gracie laughed. "Well, I appreciate that. And same here. But I doubt Bo Bixby would have saddled you with someone awful to run this place that meant so much to him."

"True indeed," he said, putting the beef into the large bowl she got for him. As he laid out his little jars of spices, he added, "Have you been giving more thought to the connection between Liam and Bo, what it could be? I have and get nowhere every time I wrack my brain."

"Same. I was talking to my best friend, Miranda, who's away for the month, about it—and I told her the whole story since I know she'll keep it to herself, and she brought up the idea of Bo having a long-lost son—Harry Ahern, Liam's father—and that Liam is Bo's grandson." Gracie shrugged. "But based on everything you said about Bo having no family and no one coming around, particularly in the last six months after he was diagnosed, that seems so unlikely. Right?"

Liam seemed to be thinking about that, and nodded. "I've wondered along those lines too. From a son he was estranged from, to a nephew he had no contact with—from an estranged brother." He also gave a shrug. "Nothing feels right about any of the scenarios, ideas. Bo was a loner and quiet, but, at heart, such a good, kind, generous person. If he had a child or a nephew or a cousin, I can't see him having turned his back on the guy."

But people do that all the time, Gracie thought.

And before she could censor herself, she said, "Liam's father seemed like a great guy to me until he found out his life would change and become very inconvenient. Granted, I only knew Harry for two months when he walked out of my life, but he *was* able to just walk away not only from me—but from the baby he knew I was carrying. I can't tell you how many times he told me he loved me while we were dating. Was he lying? Did he just feel it in the moment? Did he feel it until something changed it all for him? Like the responsibility of a child?"

She turned away for a moment, feeling tears start to sting her eyes even though she was more angry than hurt right now.

"All I know is that he left me—us," she continued. She felt herself getting more and more upset and took in a breath. "There are some people who have my trust one hundred percent—my parents and grandmother. Miranda too. But that's it. You seem like a good guy, West, but I don't know you."

He was staring at her, and her cheeks flamed.

She hadn't meant to say any of that. But out it had come and she didn't regret it. She needed to remember that she barely knew West Calhoun. That she couldn't just trust him because he *seemed* to have integrity.

He turned to her, jar of black pepper in his hand. "I understand what you're saying, Gracie. But I *did* know Bo. If he had a son, who in turn had a son, and Bo knew about the baby to leave him half the ranch, he wouldn't have just turned his back on either of the two when he was alive. I can't see it. I won't believe that. Liam's connection has to be something else."

First, West had hit a nerve in her, and now she'd hit a nerve in him.

That hadn't been her intention.

Just as she knew it hadn't been his.

Gracie watched as Liam turned back to the bowl and added spices to the ground beef, wishing they'd just stuck to cooking choices as a topic of conversation.

But some things had to be said. That they could say these things to each other—be open and honest and vulnerable—was a good thing. Even if it was overwhelming her right now. To the point that she wanted to sit down.

He stared into the bowl and shook his head, then

looked at her. "I'm sorry. I didn't mean to discount—let alone dismiss—what you said about Liam's father. I'll never understand that, Gracie, how anyone could *not* be so moved by knowing they're going to be a parent, someone's father, that it's not the most important thing in the world."

Gracie had to blink back tears. Not for herself, but for how it hit for Liam. She hated that his father hadn't felt that way. And one day, she'd have to give her child an explanation that wasn't a lie *and* wouldn't damage his heart and soul.

She couldn't even look up. Her own heart felt too heavy. And then the tears just started coming. Maybe for herself too. That a man she'd loved hadn't loved her back after all. Had been able to just walk away from her, out of her life, to avoid a future with her, a family with her.

A man she'd loved had been able to turn his back on his child. How could she have missed the signs that said, *This guy is emotionally immature*? She'd thought Harry was smart and funny and full of interesting stories about his travels for his ranch jobs. She'd felt for him that he'd lost his mother at eighteen and had no one else. When she'd ask him about his father, he'd make it clear it was a sore subject that he did not want to talk about. Gracie hadn't known if the man had died when Harry was too young to remember him or if he'd left when his mother was pregnant or when Harry was young and *did* remember. Gracie hadn't pushed because it was clear the subject bothered him, changed his mood even. Granted, she'd asked only twice, but it had been enough to know an answer wouldn't be coming.

"Gracie?" West asked gently. She could feel his gaze on her, and then suddenly he was standing right in front of her, his arms around her, pulling her into a warm embrace.

God, did it feel good.

So good that she leaned her head against his chest and let herself take the comfort he was offering.

"You know what?" she whispered, trying to stop the tears but they kept coming. "I was such an idiot about Harry Ahern that I thought when I told him I was pregnant, he'd be overjoyed. That he'd say, 'I *do* have a family. You and our baby.' How could I have judged him so wrong?"

"Hey," he said gently. "Loving someone and getting blindsided by them isn't your fault. It happens to everyone at some point or another—in a manner of ways. And it always hurts like hell."

She took in a breath, swiping under her eyes, not wanting this moment, this feeling of safety, to end.

He wrapped his arms a bit more tightly around her. "It's so hard for me to understand how people can just walk away when they're so blessed. How can they take what they have for granted like that? A beautiful, loving woman. A baby on the way. I lost my father as a kid to an accident, and then my child's mother. And people just up and leave on their own volition?"

She could feel him shaking his head, and she looked up just as he looked down.

Their lips were so close. Touching distance.

And it seemed they both had the same pull because their lips met.

He kissed her gently at first, then more passionately, tightening his hold on her.

Yes, yes, yes, she thought. *This.*

Except, a second later, her heart started beating too fast. From *fear*.

She lifted her head and put her hands on his chest to create some distance. "West."

He didn't say anything for a moment, and when she looked up at him, his eyes were closed. "I know," he finally said.

"It's a bad idea, right? This?"

The blue eyes opened slowly, full of emotion. Again, he was quiet for a few seconds. "A kiss like that, Gracie?" He let out a breath. "Passion like that leads to amazing highs and likely devastating lows. So, yes, bad idea."

Passion like that. So he'd felt it too. She was stuck on that part—instead of the second bit of what he'd said. She just wanted to sit with that kiss for a few seconds, remember it, how wonderful it had been, how special it had felt. *Passion like that* was rare.

And scary. Very scary. She could fall so hard for this man. And get hurt really badly.

Besides, for them as a couple, West Calhoun and Gracie Dawson, co-owners of the Heartland Hollows ranch, *passion like that* was plain old dangerous.

Just days ago she'd been tasked with standing in for her son's interests. And she was going to let her attraction—with its sure-to-come amazing highs and devastating lows—to his partner possibly ruin that for Liam? No.

"We both know relationships don't work out," she said, stepping back, then pulling completely out of the embrace and making a show of getting out the Italian bread. To have something to do with her hands. With her attention.

West clearly had the same idea because he washed his hands, then began forming the meatballs and dropping them into the sauce in the pan. He kept his gaze on his job.

"And if we give in to this," she said, putting the loaf of bread, still in its wrapping, onto a plate. "We'll eventually start having issues and arguments."

"And then suddenly partners running a multimillion-dollar operation aren't speaking," he said.

Yes, exactly. "I know that Heartland Hollows isn't about the bottom line to you, West. It's about Bo and the heart and soul he put into this place. Kissing—and wherever that leads—puts all that in jeopardy. In Bo's memory and Liam's future."

He dropped his head back a bit, then turned to look at her. "I agree a hundred percent. But—"

But? There couldn't be a but.

He let out a breath—and held her gaze. "*But* you're so damned beautiful, Gracie. And easy to talk to. And you were very nice to my kid. Not to mention a hundred other very good adjectives that describe you—and I barely know you. That's the but. I don't want less of you. I want *more*."

Oh, West. She almost lost her resolve right there,

wanting so badly to hurry back into his embrace, have those strong arms around her again, her head against his hard chest, his heart beating underneath.

Instead, she flashed back to the days after it was clear that Harry had left her—for good. When she'd discovered he'd blocked her. That she had no way to get in touch with him. That he had no interest in ever hearing from her again. Or about their child.

The pain she'd been in. The crying. Her poor parents and grandmother, casting worried, sorrowful looks at one another as they brought her tissues and sat with her. Days on end.

When she should have been celebrating that she was pregnant, that she was going to be a mother as she'd always dreamed of, she'd been brokenhearted and scared and panicked.

That was also what love wrought.

Be smart, Gracie. For Liam.

The resolve was back, full force. "I'm not gonna act like that didn't mean a lot to me, West. It did. All of it. But that's just another reason why we should draw the line here," she said. "Right now, we have a really good professional relationship. Let's not get to know each other better—on a personal level. For the ranch. For Alexa and Liam's futures."

Let's not get to know each other better... It managed to hang heavy in the air between them, at least for her. What an awful thing to have to say to someone.

Someone she wished she could know better, she thought, her heart splintering. She wanted more too. Much more.

"So that was our first and last kiss," he said, adding a very soft smile. Because she *had* gotten to know him more on a personal level, she knew he was saying he was on the same page. That it was hard for him too. She could feel everything he was thinking. "At least it was a doozy."

She couldn't help but smile. West always knew what to say to help her along.

Because he knows you on a personal level.
And you're both shutting that down? Huh?
This is what people dream of. The amazing passion. The knowing each other. The sensitivity.

And they were calling it. Ending things before they even began.

This isn't right either, she thought glumly. *But it needs to be this way.*

He spooned some sauce over the meatballs, then moved over to where he'd set the box of spaghetti. Then he made a show of reading the directions, which she doubted was really necessary. It was clear he needed to create a little emotional distance to go with the physical.

Finally, he looked at her. "I've had the same thoughts about why something between us would be complicated. I know it's not a good idea."

"So…friends. Partners."

"Friends and partners," he said with a nod. The gentle smile again.

But as they looked at each other, all she felt was a yearning for more. And she saw the same in his eyes, in his expression, in his body language.

Chapter Eight

Instead of being able to fully enjoy a baby clearly loving his first bite of meatball—and West's generations-old family recipe—he was very distracted. Not about what he and Gracie had just basically shaken on—to be platonic. No, he was stuck on the kiss and unable to stop thinking about it. Remembering it. Reliving it. Especially with her sitting across from him at the kitchen table.

That had been no ordinary kiss—ordinary being the kind he'd had at the end of several great first dates the past ten years. Ordinary because he'd been aware something was missing right there in the middle of it. Either an emotional spark or a lust spark, when he'd felt one or both on the date itself. He'd know the relationship would peter out in a few weeks, a few months, and it always did. He'd wonder if he was putting too much stock into a first kiss, but it felt telltale, a predictor. He'd kissed his late wife for the first time and cymbals had sounded in his head, fireworks in his heart.

Kissing Gracie Dawson was like that.

Which scared him like hell. He knew had feelings for her. But...

How was he supposed to put that kiss out of his head and think of Gracie as solely a friend and partner?

She was a step ahead of him because she turned the conversation to Liam's first taste of meatball, and how delicious West's specialty was.

"You weren't kidding about how good this is," she said, her green eyes happy again as she twirled pasta on her fork. "I could live on spaghetti and meatballs, but only scrumptious ones like these." She ate her bite, letting out a satisfied sigh. Then she turned to her son, beside the table in his high chair. "And you so agree, Liam!" she said, placing another small piece of meatball on his baby spoon and offering it to him. He took it eagerly.

West laughed. "Ah, I could watch that all day. A baby discovering he loves Italian food. And my cooking." His tiny partner was a constant source of a joy. Who'd have seen that coming?

Gracie laughed, too, the earlier tension dissipated if not gone. They were both trying, clearly, and with the focus on anything but them, it was working. Once Liam had eaten his fill and was happily batting at nothing and letting out the occasional babble, she turned to her phone and a list of questions about Heartland Hollows. Smart move. There was a lot they hadn't talked about so far, such as how they'd arrange their hours as co-owners, and that was first on her list.

They decided each would be "on duty" when they were least needed at home. For West, that was between 8:30 and 3:00 p.m., allowing time in the morning to have breakfast with his daughter and walk her to the bus. And since Liam tended to wake at 5:30 a.m. like clockwork every day, Gracie preferred to have those early hours with him. So West would be on duty from 5:30 to 7:00 a.m., when he'd go home to make sure Alexa wasn't hitting the snooze button too many times.

This would work out perfectly for both of them. During the week, Gracie's mom, an early riser herself, would come over from 7:00 to 8:30 a.m. to watch her grandson while Gracie got the morning chores done—ones that couldn't be easily performed with a baby in a chest carrier or parked in a corner where she couldn't pay attention to him. Apparently they'd made these arrangements the day Gracie had moved into the ranch house. The rest of the working hours, she and West would split.

"And on my off hours," he said, "I'm happy to babysit my favorite little guy if there's something you need to get done on the ranch or off."

Gracie stared at him as if in shock, piece of Italian bread paused in the air. "What? Really?"

He took his final bite of swirled spaghetti and sat back. "We're a team, Gracie. The *three* of us. So, of course. I know my way around babies. And helping you out with watching him lets you have time to really dig into this place the way you want since you won't have to worry about Liam or what time it is. If something comes up, we'll find a solution."

She was shaking her head as if in wonder now. "I have a couple of sitters I can call if need be," she said with a nod. "But wow, West. You said you didn't know how *you* got so lucky with me and Liam as co-owner, but I'd say he and I are the lucky ones. I'm so grateful for how accommodating you are."

He touched her hand for second then drew it back the second he remembered. Not even casual gestures of thanks or appreciation. No hand squeezes, no arm slung around her shoulder.

If he wasn't mistaken, she'd noticed.

"We're very lucky, indeed, Mr. Big Cheeks," she said to Liam, leaning over to give him a kiss on the head.

Defusing again. Taking the focus off them, off how that second-long touch had affected both of them.

His phone rang, another welcome distraction in the moment. As she scooped up Liam and settled a burp cloth over her shoulder, he grabbed his phone.

It was Alexa.

"Hey, honey, how's studying going?" She was probably going to ask if she could stay another half hour.

He heard sniffling. Wait—was she *crying*? Then she whispered, "Dad, can you come get me? Everyone's mad at me." Her voice broke and she was clearly crying now. "Can Gracie come too?"

His heart had seized up with the sniffles alone. "Alexa, I'll be right there."

"Can Gracie come with you?" she repeated.

He eyed Gracie, who was looking at him with compassion as she gave Liam a rock in her arms. "If she can, sweetheart. See you in five minutes." He disconnected. He told her what Alexa had said and sounded like.

"Let's go," she said. "It'll take just a few seconds to get Liam in a fleece and cap for the car ride."

"They're mad at her?" he asked. "And by 'they,' I'm assuming she means the girls at the study party. Her two best friends, Riley and Lauren. What the hell could have happened in two and a half hours while studying for a history unit test on the Roaring Twenties?"

He couldn't imagine. There was no hint of anything remotely wrong in Alexa Calhoun's life this morning. As he'd told Gracie, she'd gone happily off to school with her hair wavy from a little time with the curling iron again this morning. Without the glittering eye shadow and sparkly lip gloss, she'd looked like his daughter again—the one he recognized. She'd looked like a kid with a little hair flair. It had been clear she was happy with how she looked and she'd even mentioned she couldn't wait to show her friends her hair.

As he and Gracie headed to the door, West grabbed his keys from the console bowl, and Gracie, getting Liam into his fleece, said, "You know, because she asked for me to come with you, I would have thought she'd gotten her period for the first time. But the part about her friends being mad at her makes that a no."

West could feel his eyes widen. "Her period," he said kind of numbly. "That subject hasn't come up at all, so I don't think she's gotten it. But, yeah, makes sense that it's something else. But what? Why would her friends be mad at her all of a sudden?"

They were in her SUV in moments, Liam settled in his rear-facing car seat, and then they headed down the drive.

"I should have talked to her about that stuff—periods,

puberty," he said as he turned onto the road into town. "She's *twelve*, which means I'm late. I have a little here and there, but I've never sat down and said, 'Alexa, let's talk about the birds and the bees.' I guess certain topics like that have just come up organically, like how babies are made, but she doesn't really like to talk about it with me."

"They do cover the subject in school, in the health portion of PE. And her friends have likely talked about it a lot. Plus, there's Google. But as her sole parent, yeah, it *is* a conversation for Dad to have with her, to make sure she knows the basics, to answer any questions. She may say, '*Dad*,' and run away, but she'll know she can ask you anything."

He nodded. "I'll do that in the next few days, once this little fire is put out. *If* it's little. What can seem small to me is huge to her. I've learned that."

Gracie touched her hand to his forearm in what he took as solidarity, but then she withdrew it quickly, as he'd done earlier. He sighed.

Nothing like being on the same page about something so...weird. Complicated.

"I can't imagine what could have happened at the study party," he said. "Quizzing each other and... what? Maybe Alexa grabbed the last pepperoni slice in the box. Maybe she dropped a cupcake on one of the girl's feet."

"The speculation will drive you bonkers. You'll find out in a few minutes."

"Except I'm not sure I want to know. Alexa's been

close with these girls since middle school started last year. I've never gotten a call like this."

They pulled into Riley's driveway, and the front door of the colonial opened. Alexa, looking like she might burst into tears at any moment, her backpack slung over one shoulder, stood there with Riley's mom, Gabrielle Pemerton.

"Be right back," he said and hurried to the door, looking from his daughter's sad, nervous downcast face and her friend's mother.

"There seems to have been a disagreement among the girls and Alexa decided she'd like to go home," Gabrielle said. She looked so much like her daughter with their auburn hair and hazel eyes. But the two girls weren't around. She leaned closer and whispered, "I tried to talk to them about it but they were all so cagey."

"Did you want to say goodbye to your friends?" he asked his daughter, just in case having Dad suggest it might lead to a reconciliation.

"I just want to go home," Alexa barely whispered, staring at her shoes.

Gabrielle smiled at him. "I'm sure they'll work it out."

He thanked her, and before he even turned, Alexa had shot to the car, peering into the passenger seat. West saw her visibly relax at the sight of Gracie, then hurry into the back seat.

West got in and buckled up.

"Liam's eyes are all droopy," Alexa said, and West could tell she was barely holding it together.

Gracie turned, her expression compassionate. "It's getting very close to his bedtime."

Alexa burst into tears, covering her face with her hands. "My friends hate me. I'm out of the group."

West's heart seized up again. She'd never said anything like that before. He glanced at Gracie. She twisted more fully in her seat so she could see Alexa.

"Honey, I'm assuming there was an argument," Gracie said. "What happened?"

Alexa swiped under her eyes, sniffling. "Dad, don't listen, okay? I want to tell Gracie."

"I'm right here, though, sweetheart. But go ahead and talk to Gracie." He tried not to glance in the rearview mirror to give his daughter at least the semblance of privacy.

Alexa scooted as far over to the side as her seat belt would allow so that he couldn't see her face anymore. "Riley and Lauren decided they want to wear their hair pin-straight for the dance, but I want mine wavy. They said I have to flat-iron mine like theirs so we match."

"Why do you have to match?" West asked before he remembered he wasn't even supposed to be listening.

She was staring down. "Because we decided last week that we're matching for the dance. But they changed everything today without even telling me until the pizza came. They want to totally change what dresses we're wearing too. Instead of the same dress in different colors that we got in Brewer last weekend, they want us all to wear the red dresses we wore to last year's holiday party at school."

West eyed Gracie, who he could see was trying to hide her frown. A hard frown.

"I see," Gracie said, looking as though she was taking everything in. "Honey, what did you mean by you're out of the group?"

"I told them I wanted to wear my hair wavy and my purple dress and that we don't *have* to match. And they said if we don't match, then I'm not in the group."

Not in the group. What the hell? Over a hairstyle and a dress? *What?*

Alexa started crying again. "And they said that we can't be friends anymore. 'Your choice,' Riley said to me. And she was staring really hard at me. Lauren was too. I didn't know what to say. So I said I had a stomachache and needed to leave early."

Oh, Alexa. Would this stuff ever end? Or would middle schoolers suffer through this crap till the end of time?

West wanted to pull over and turn to face his daughter to tell her if her friends cared more about wearing their hair all the same than about being her friend, then they were hardly good friends. But there was a reason Alexa had wanted Gracie to be here for this; when it came to seventh-grade friendships, yammering on with a life lesson on what made a friend wasn't going to help right now.

"I also wanted to add a purple stripe in my hair for the dance, and they said that would look way too matchy-matchy with my dress and nails, and was totally stupid anyway, so it was good that they changed the plan."

"What do you think about all this, Alexa?" Gracie asked.

He could lean over and kiss Gracie for immediately going to that. Of course that was the question to ask. And West wouldn't have thought of it. He might have bulldozed on about the meaning of true friends—before after realizing he shouldn't.

"I think it's so unfair!" she yelled and then started crying again. She turned to her left, where the baby was in the rear-facing car seat "Sorry for yelling, Liam. He's sleeping. I didn't wake him up."

"That's okay, honey," Alexa said.

West turned into the drive for the ranch then pulled up in front of Gracie's house.

Gracie turned in her seat to face his daughter. "Alexa, I'd love your help getting Liam ready for bed if you don't have to hurry home."

The woman was gold.

West glanced in the rearview mirror. The relief on his daughter's face—and the way her eyes brightened—made his heart skip a beat.

"If that's all right, West," Gracie added.

"Fine with me," he said.

"Like a mother's helper?" Alexa said, a little life coming back into her voice. "I've never gotten a baby ready for bed before. Is it hard?"

Gracie smiled. "Nope. Well, sometimes Liam can be a fusspot if he's overtired or if he's fighting sleep because he wants another story. But mostly, after his bottle and a bath, cuddly pj's and a story, he's falls right to sleep. But no worries, I'll show you what to do."

Alexa actually smiled, her gaze on the baby in Gracie's arms. "I wonder if I'd be good at helping. I hope so."

"I'm sure you'll be great," Gracie said. "Liam already adores you."

He saw a little spirit in his daughter's face at that. He wouldn't have thought anything could distract Alexa from her problems with her friends, but Gracie definitely had the magic touch here and he'd let her handle this as she saw fit.

As they went into the house, Alexa was asking Gracie questions about what kinds of stories Liam liked and how she could tell if he didn't like one. West trailed behind, giving them some space. Once again, he owed Gracie Dawson.

"Make yourself at home," Gracie said to West while Alexa was standing by the fireplace and looking at the photos on the mantel. "Alexa and I will be upstairs getting Liam ready for bed." *And talking*, she didn't need to add. "And then we'll read him a story. He'll love the extra kiss good-night too."

Alexa whirled around with a smile. "I've never read a baby a story before."

West smiled at his daughter then looked at Gracie, nodding in understanding. "If you don't mind, I'd like to start going through Bo's desk in the office. It's the one room I didn't poke around in, since I figured we'd do that together. But I can get started while you two are upstairs."

Now she was reading into what *he* wasn't saying—in front of Alexa. That maybe he'd find something connecting Bo to Liam in the office. She remembered that West didn't want to tell Alexa that the baby was actually the co-owner until they got to the bottom of that mystery.

"Sure," she said. "I'll look through, too, later tonight." She smiled at him, then turned to Alexa. "Ready for baby land?"

Alexa was still smiling. "Yes!"

This was a good sign. That being a mother's helper was such a fun and exciting prospect for Alexa that it had pulled her from her problems with her friends. Maybe it was a way to cope, but it was a good way. They'd talk and hopefully Alexa would find some peace with the situation. Getting kicked out of your friend group was serious stuff, even for a night, and very painful.

They headed upstairs and into the nursery. Gracie had given Liam a bath before dinner since he'd been so fussy and he loved the feeling of warm fragrant bubbles on his skin. He'd calmed down after that and had been a perfect dinner cohost—and eater of his first meatball. She almost thought about sharing that detail with Alexa but thought better of it. It might sound like a date to Alexa, and she didn't want to put that in the girl's head. Especially not when she had enough to contend with right now.

"Liam's room is so sweet," Alexa said, her gaze on the teddy bear on his changing table. Then she burst into tears, hands flying to cover her face, and stood there crying.

Gracie set Liam sitting up in his crib with a chew

toy, then rushed over to Alexa and took her hand. "I'm so sorry you're going through this. Tell me more about what happened, honey." She led Alexa over to the two chairs that she'd brought in from the guest room yesterday and was now very glad she had. They sat down, Alexa dropping her face into her hands.

The girl launched into the story in more detail. Apparently, the two girls had had a weird reaction to Alexa's wavy hair and were cool to her all day, then at the study party had said they'd changed their minds about their look for the dance, including their dresses and they were now going to wear red dresses since it was more holidayesque. When Alexa had insisted on sticking to the original plan—all of them with wavy hair and wearing the similar dresses they'd bought just last weekend, each in a different color that they loved, with matching nails and friendship bracelets—they'd told her she thought she was better than they were because her father now owned the Heartland Hollows Ranch.

Oh, Alexa. Gracie well remembered this kind of thing from middle school. The jabs, big and small. And being dumped by a close friend.

Tears streamed down Alexa's face. She lifted her face slightly to wipe at her eyes. "I would have said okay too. But…" She clammed up and stared out the window.

"But," Gracie prompted gently.

Alexa sniffled and looked down at the rug. "But… my mother's favorite color was dark purple. Plum. So wearing a dark purple dress and nails felt like…" She buried her face again, sobbing.

Gracie's heart clenched. She moved closer to Alexa and put an arm around her. "I can understand why sticking to the original plan was important to you. That's a very special, sweet reason to wear purple. You'd probably feel like your mom was with you at your very first school dance."

Alexa looked at Gracie and nodded, the girl barely able to hold it together. Her bottom lip was trembling. "And my mom had wavy hair, too, but I got my dad's straight hair. In my favorite picture of her holding me, when we were at a lake cabin vacation, my mom's hair is long and wavy like mine is today."

Gracie's heart was squeezing in her chest for this sweet girl.

"They were like, 'Why are you making a big deal about this?' So I even told them why and Riley said, 'I'm sorry about your mom, but come on, Alexa. That's not fair to me and Lauren.' And so I just said, 'Well, I really want to wear my purple dress and my hair wavy.' I didn't say it in a mean way or anything. But they told me I was out of the group because we wouldn't match."

How stupid. How completely stupid. They were going to turn their backs on their good friend, even after she'd explained her poignant reasoning for wanting to stick to the plan, over a dress and hairstyle? What the—

"So now I don't have any friends," Alexa said, tears streaming down her face again. "I was pretty much on my own before this year," she managed to say, her voice cracking. "I had a couple of friends in classes to say hi to, but this was the first time I belonged to a group. And I really liked it." She burst into tears again and dropped her head down.

"I know just how you feel," Gracie said. "Something similar happened to me in eighth grade."

Alexa looked up and grabbed a tissue from the box on the little round table between the chairs. She wiped at her eyes with the backs of her hands. "Really? What happened? How did it end up?"

"It was awful. I cried my eyes out too. A girl I thought was my best friend got really mad at me because someone told her I liked the same boy she liked and had been seen talking to him by his locker and outside at recess. I told her I didn't like him at all and she said, 'Why, you don't think he's cute?' It just got worse from there. I don't know if the girl was trying to break up our friendship for some reason or what. But my best friend never spoke to me again, and she became besties with the girl who lied. I hated going to school every day and seeing them walking around. And sometimes matching, too, like socks or shirt colors."

"Did you make a new best friend?" Alexa asked, her face so hopeful.

"Not right away," she said honestly. "But my lab partner in science class, who I never really even talked to much before, invited me to study for our final at her house, and within a few months, we were best friends and are to this day. Her name's Miranda. In fact, thanks to her, I ended up going to 4-H camp and I made even more friends—and I found out how much I love farming and ranching and working with animals."

Alexa brightened a bit. She seemed to be taking all

that in. Hopefully, a little comforted that if Gracie had made a new best friend and then wonderful things had happened, maybe it would be the same for her.

"I wonder if Riley and Lauren really won't be friends with me anymore. Maybe they'll call tonight and say it's okay if I wear purple and wavy hair."

"Well, it *is* okay if you do. But I know you know that."

Alexa frowned hard. "Yeah, but I also know it's not going to be okay with them. I could tell they meant it."

"What do you think about that?"

Alexa shrugged. "I know what my dad would say."

Gracie smiled to herself. "Oh, yeah? What would he say?"

"That they're not *good* friends." She sighed and her face fell again, but she didn't cry, another good sign. She seemed buoyed by Gracie's own sorry tale of middle school heartache. "I want them to still like me, though."

"I know," Gracie said. "But what your dad would say is definitely right. They're not being *good* friends to you."

Alexa hung her head, looking so sad. "They both have moms. So they just don't get it."

Oh, honey, Gracie thought. She was out of her depth here. She didn't want to say the wrong thing. Or what she should say just because she was the grownup in the room. All she could do was speak from the heart.

"Want to know what I think?" Gracie asked, crossing her fingers.

Alexa stared at her, waiting.

"I think you're the only one who has to get it. Because it matters to *you*."

Alexa tilted her head and bit her lip. She seemed to be thinking about that. "I guess I'm not going to the dance anyway, though. So…"

"You *could* go. In your plum dress and matching nails and your wavy hair. Your mom will be with you the whole time. Proud of her girl. Proud of who you are, Alexa Calhoun."

Alexa's gaze shot to Gracie, a slight gasp coming from her. "Do you think so?" Her eyes were wide and teary.

"Yes, I do. One hundred percent."

Alexa flew at Gracie, wrapping her in a hug, physically awkward given Gracie was sitting in an armchair, but it still felt wonderful. "I really like thinking that my mom would be proud of me," she added, sitting back on her own chair.

"Ba wa!" came a little voice from the crib.

Alexa laughed. "Aww, Liam is lonely."

"If you want to keep an eye on him for a few minutes, I'll go make his bedtime bottle. You can feed him, then we'll change him and settle him into bed with a story."

Alexa's eyes lit up. "I can watch him myself?"

"Sure can. I'll be right downstairs in the kitchen and back in three minutes." Gracie smiled.

Alexa's face brightened and Gracie walked her over to the crib. "What should I do?"

"Just keep an eye on him. He'll probably just keeping doing what he's doing right now—staring at you."

That got a laugh from Alexa, which was very nice to hear.

"And if he starts screaming his head off," Gracie said, "I'll hear him and come right up, okay? Otherwise, back in a few with his bottle." Gracie put a hand on Alexa's shoulder and then hurried down the stairs. Along the way, she let out one heck of a breath.

Whew, she thought. *That wasn't easy. No wonder West gets tied in knots.*

In the kitchen, there was the man himself, making a pot of coffee. Not even decaf.

"I thought I'd need the caffeine boost," West said as he saw her coming through the doorway. "Is she all right?"

"You know what? I think she is. Hurt and stung and sad, definitely. But sure in her stance. I'll let her tell you about it. She's a great girl, West."

Now *his* face brightened. "Offering to make you a cup of coffee seems hardly adequate for whatever magic you worked upstairs." He took her hand and held her gaze, the sincerity and appreciation making her wish she could rush into his arms and hold him.

How was she going to get through tonight without wanting to kiss him again, let alone the next twenty years?

"Honestly, I just did a lot of listening," Gracie said. "Right now, she's watching Liam for a few minutes while I make a bottle."

"Ah, perfect. I'll run up and just say hi, let her know without saying anything that I'm here for her."

She grabbed a clean bottle from the cabinet and got to work. "You're a great dad, West," she said, looking at him as he leaned against the counter, his coffee mug wrapped in both hands. "My father was a little more on the silent side when I was growing up and left all talks to my mom, but there were a few times when he'd ask if I wanted to go fishing or to a petting zoo when he knew I was out of sorts about something, and I always felt his love. I always felt how much he cared."

"I like that. A lot," he said, taking a sip of coffee.

"And you're right there. You put yourself out there in ways that make me hope I'll be as present for my child." She gave the bottle a shake, her heart doing strange things in her chest. Surging, then retreating.

He looked right at her, his blue eyes so warm. She wanted another one of his hugs. But those were off the table. Dammit. "You have no idea what that means to me. I always think I'm ruining everything. What did I do before you arrived?" He shook his head in wonder.

In another time and place, one of them would step toward the other for another very passionate kiss, taking all these feelings, this attraction, this beautiful connection, to the next level.

But that couldn't happen, and Gracie didn't like it. Not at all. There was nothing she wanted more right now than to be in West Calhoun's arms.

"I'll head up and see her," he said.

The moment he turned and left the room, she felt his absence acutely. It was becoming clear to her that she needed West in ways she wasn't allowed to have him.

So what was she supposed to do with that?

Chapter Nine

"Hey," West said gently from the doorway of the nursery.

Alexa turned with a shy smile. "Gracie said I could watch Liam while she's making his bottle. I'm a real mother's helper now."

"That you are." It took all his willpower not to go to her and wrap his arms around his little girl and tell her he'd make everything okay. She wasn't a little girl anymore. And he couldn't make this okay. He could just try to be wise and insightful and not say the wrong thing.

What he had to do was be there for her, like Gracie had always felt her dad was. He wanted Alexa to grow up knowing he *was* there. And always would be.

"I'm a little scared to be alone with him because he's so little," Alexa said, looking from Liam to him, "but because Gracie is just downstairs, I'm not worried. I can always call her if he starts crying."

West nodded with a smile. "When you were a fussbudget as a baby, your mom and I would sing to you and seventy-five percent of the time, you'd stop crying."

She sucked in a breath and kept her glance on the baby, her eyes getting misty.

"You okay, Lex?"

She sniffled a bit. "You said dark purple was Mom's favorite color." And then she told him about the group's dress code for the dance—and how Riley and Lauren had changed it. "And they're wearing totally straight hair. But…"

"But you want to wear your hair like your mom's. Wavy."

She nodded and started crying in earnest, his heart breaking for her, the rest of the story coming out slowly in her cracking voice.

He pulled his daughter into a hug and held her tight. "I like that you told them how you feel and why it was important to you to stick to the plan. I'm really proud of you, Lex."

She sniffled again and he loosened his hold, sensing she needed a little space. She bit her lip and moved closer to the crib, her gaze on the baby. "I was thinking I couldn't even go to the dance, but Gracie said that by wearing plum and having waves in my hair, it would be like my mom is with me and that she'd be proud of me too."

She brightened a bit. "Do you think she would be?" She was looking at him shyly, with such hope in her face that West just wanted to pull her into another hug and never let her go.

If West's heart had been moving in his chest a minute ago, now it was about to burst. "She would be very proud of you, Lex. Very proud of the girl her daughter is. I know that more than I know anything."

Alexa smiled then, a real smile. "After Gracie said

that, I thought I might even go to the dance alone even though I don't have friends. She said something similar happened to her and she made a new best friend. She even found out what she wanted to do with her life. Gracie's so nice."

"She is," he said, his chest squeezing.

Thank you, Gracie. Thank you.

"And she *is* a great mom, just like you said when I got upset the other day."

He smiled gently and rested his head atop hers.

"If you married Gracie, she'd be my stepmother," she said, not looking at him.

He lifted his head—in total shock.

Married Gracie? Where had that come from? Who said anything about marriage?

"Gracie and I aren't a couple, though," he pointed out very necessarily despite her sudden frown. "We're business partners."

"Well, if you did get married, I'd be happy about that. I know two girls who hate their dad's girlfriends."

He managed a smile, but the sudden turn in conversation had caught him completely off guard. He wrapped his daughter in another fierce hug. "You're a smart, kind, beautiful, interesting person with a huge heart, Alexa Dawson. I love you. And I'm happy that you're my daughter."

"You *have* to say that," she said, but she was smiling. Suddenly, the smile faded. "I'm scared about going to school tomorrow. We always meet by Riley's locker before the first bell. And we always sit together at lunch." Tears misted her eyes again.

"That's gonna be rough, honey. No way around it. I think the only thing you can do is feel proud for sticking up for yourself, for knowing that when something is very important to you, you go with it."

"That's true, Dad," she said, wiping under her eyes. "It makes me feel better to think of it that way. It's for Mom." The light was back in her face again.

"For Mom," he whispered, kissing the top of her head.

For a moment, they just stood there, not speaking, just *feeling*. He knew he'd treasure this talk, these minutes, forever.

"I'm back," said a voice from the doorway as Gracie came in with a bottle.

"I'll let you get back to being a mother's helper," West said. He gave Alexa's hand a squeeze and then mouthed a *Thank you* to Gracie as he passed her on his way out.

Tonight likely would have gone very differently had West handled it on his own.

Gracie smiled back at him, and something shifted inside him, something worrying.

He was falling for this woman. This woman who'd helped his daughter out of a highly charged emotional jam in a way that astounded him.

She was gold.

But she couldn't be his. *You two shook on a deal to keep things platonic.* No kissing. And certainly not more, despite his thoughts and fantasies going off in many delicious directions.

If you married Gracie, she'd be my stepmother...

He had introduced three girlfriends to Alexa over the years, forcing himself on a few casual outings for ice cream or the petting zoo at the Dawson Family Guest Ranch. Alexa had been curious about the women and had asked if he was going to marry them, and he'd been honest that they were just dating, which had made her seem relieved. Certainly none had lasted more than a few months because he couldn't get himself to commit. Exclusivity—fine, as they'd gotten to know each other. But no one had gotten him thinking about next levels.

Now here was his daughter basically giving her approval of Gracie as a stepmother.

He'd asked her a few times if she liked the idea of him getting married and she always said she didn't know. He'd said, *Me either*, and she'd laughed.

But now, with Gracie, everything was different. His reaction to her. Alexa's reaction to her.

But, but, but. One major argument, and then a slew of them, and their romance would be over. Then things would get easily awkward between Gracie and his daughter; he could see her unsure as how to proceed with a big shift in her relationship with him, and things getting very weird.

Keeping things on a friends level would also protect Alexa's relationship with Gracie, who would be a big part of her life for at least the next five to six years while she was still in school. Alexa would always call Heartland Hollows home, no matter where life might take her after high school. Whether college or a job or a move to a new place entirely. If something went wrong between him and Gracie, the tension, the complications, the big problems, couldn't possibly be worth taking even a baby step toward a relationship. No matter how much they liked each other. Or wanted each other.

He went downstairs with a hard sigh, poured himself another cup of coffee in the kitchen, and then headed into the office.

Just sitting at the mahogany desk with its intricately carved legs and the large matching leather chair had West missing his friend and boss and mentor, the man who'd taught him so much.

Loving someone gets you this, he was reminded. *Grief-stricken. Feeling like hell. Like a piece of you is missing and you can't replace it.*

That he and Gracie needed to be platonic was like a blessing in disguise. These new feelings he had for her meant a breakup—an inevitable breakup because what lasted?—would destroy him. He wasn't going there.

Be the father your daughter needs. The owner this ranch needs.

Which reminded him why he was in this chair, at this desk. To go through the drawers, find something that would link Bo to Liam Dawson. Something. Anything.

He took a bracing sip of the coffee, then opened the top drawer. Bo had kept his records on his laptop, which West now had at home, and he'd already shared all those files with Gracie. So whatever was in the drawers was more of a personal nature or whatever hard copies he might have of this or that. West felt funny about poking through Bo's desk, but then again, anything Bo didn't want anyone's eyes on, he would have taken care of in his final month, for sure.

There were three drawers on each side of the desk. The left side was empty. Top right was empty. Middle empty. But there was a small, flat manila envelope in the third drawer. Nothing written on it.

West picked it up. It wasn't sealed. Inside he found a photograph—on the grainy side, whether just an off shot or an old photo, he wasn't sure. The subject was a little kid, maybe four or five, with a cowboy hat on his head, a blue T-shirt and jeans and orange sneakers. He stood in front of bushes and what looked like a fence. But not a ranch fence. More like chain-link.

West studied it closely. The boy had been photographed from a distance. West peered closely at the photo, looking for any personalization on the kid's clothes, a name or initials on the T-shirt or hat. Nothing. Nothing about the bushes or fencing gave away its location either.

Why would Bo Bixby have an old photo of a little kid in his desk?

Because he *did* have family? Because this child was a relation? The son who kept coming up as a possibility? West wasn't sure. The boy in the photo could be Bo himself as a kid. A brother who died young who Bo couldn't bear to talk about. He could be the child of anyone who might have been important to Bo at some point in time, enough that he'd kept the photo.

He could be Harry Ahern, Liam's father.

Bo had clearly gone through his desk in his final

month and gotten rid of what wasn't necessary for the ranch since there was nothing in the drawers but that envelope containing the photo. He'd left it behind for a reason. Either he hadn't known what to do with it or he'd wanted it to be found.

As explanation? Because the boy *was* Harry Ahern? And Liam *was* Harry's son? And the reason Bo had left Liam half the ranch. It made the most sense.

And the least.

God, this was so frustrating.

Why would Bo say he had no family if he had a son—who'd been alive and well until a few months after Liam Dawson was born?

Had Bo ever actually said the words *I don't have children*? Or had he only ever used the word *family*? West tried to remember—but couldn't. Maybe Bo had differentiated. Having family meant connection to people. And for some reason, that hadn't existed for Bo Bixby.

So perhaps the two—Harry Ahern and Bo Bixby—had been estranged. Maybe even very early on in Harry's life. A son, but no family bond?

Maybe the estrangement went back to childhood, something to do with Harry's mother? Gracie might know something more about the woman, though it sounded as though she didn't. West recalled her saying that Harry had also said he'd had no family after his mother died when he was eighteen. Perhaps because of an estranged father? Maybe. And maybe not.

They'd have to do some digging.

He looked at the photo, staring hard for any likeness to Liam, but the little boy was just too far away for that.

All that connected the little kid to Liam's father was that Bo had left Liam Dawson half the ranch for a good reason no one knew yet. And he was wearing a cowboy hat—a sign that he'd been in a ranching family then. Or part of one. For a time, anyway.

So many questions and no answers.

He'd show Gracie the photo in the morning, on his way back from walking Alexa to the bus stop. Right now wasn't the time to burst upstairs with it. He didn't want to shift the focus from his daughter tonight. Liam was likely close to sleep, and then he and Alexa would head to the cabin and call it a very long day. She might want to talk more about what had happened with her friends, about her mother, and he wanted a clear head for that.

Besides, he and Gracie weren't going to figure out the mysterious link tonight anyway. And once again, he had more questions than answers. Which felt like the story of his life at the moment.

I found an old photo of a little kid—a boy—in Bo's desk last night. Drawers were otherwise empty. I can stop by with it now if the timing is good for you.

Her heart had sped up at West's text and she'd responded immediately that now was perfect. Liam was sitting in his playpen, holding his squishy bunny with ears that were chewable. Holding on to an object was a new milestone, and he was staring at the toy in absolute wonder.

She'd wanted to see that photo, see if it was Harry. Whenever Gracie looked at photos of herself or even her parents as little kids, she could see their faces. Surely she'd recognize Harry Ahern if the boy was him.

With a manila envelope in his hand, West was now leaning against her kitchen counter, near where they'd stood last night, cooking, talking, sharing, eating—kissing. For a moment, that was all she could think about.

Everything about last night had made her feel so close to him, from dinner and the kiss, to the agreement to *not* kiss, to be platonic, to Alexa's call.

Can Gracie come too?

And all that had happened back here, upstairs. How Alexa had opened up about her mother. How, somehow, Gracie had found the right words.

She felt close to *both* Calhouns. Double trouble. And she had so many questions for West about how the rest of the night had gone with Alexa, how this morning had gone.

"First, let me ask about Alexa," Gracie said. "How was she when you two got home last night? Did she talk more about the fight with her friends? Or supposed friends, I should say."

When he'd mouthed *Thank you* last night as she'd come back upstairs with Liam's bottle, she had a feeling Alexa had opened up to her dad a little.

West nodded. "She told me the basics when I was in the nursery with her while you were making Liam's bottle. About the significance of the color of the dress and the wavy hair. And what you said about it all." He shook his head, as if in wonder, and she was instantly touched. "How are you so good at this with your six months of experience?"

Gracie laughed. "I was a twelve-year-old girl once."

"I'm lucky you're here," he said. "You're a gift, Gracie Dawson."

That went straight to her heart, where it crept into nooks and crannies and couldn't be dislodged no matter how hard she tried.

Between what he'd said and the sincerity in his expression, she felt shy suddenly, too aware of him and how he affected her. She stood up, trying to get a little control of herself, and pointed to the coffeepot on the counter. "Coffee?"

"I'll get it. You can check out the photo," he said, setting the envelope on the table next to her own mug of coffee.

She nodded, then sat back down and stared at the envelope—which might finally hold the answer they'd been after since the reading of the will.

She took a sip of her coffee and finally slid out the photo, holding it close to study it. She couldn't immediately identify the boy as Harry. The photo was grainy and the boy wore a cowboy hat, so she couldn't even tell if he had brown hair like Harry. Sandy-brown. Forget the eye color—Gracie couldn't discern. Harry's had been blue, like Liam's. Like Bo's, per the photos she'd seen of him.

That the photo had been taken from a distance didn't help.

She turned it over. Nothing written on the back. "Huh. The photo looks old, but not majorly dated. I can't see the boy's hair to find clues in the style, but his clothes and sneakers look pretty recent—meaning the last twenty-five, thirty years?"

"Agreed," he said, coming over with his coffee and eyeing the photo.

"Yeah, this could be one of my cousins as a four- to six-year-old. Which means the age may be right to be Harry Ahern, Liam's father. He was twenty-nine, same as me. *Could* this be him?" She brought the photo even closer, then held it away, then brought it closer. "I was hoping I'd know right away if it was Harry, but I can't tell. It *could* be."

She set it down on top of the envelope and stared at it while she took another long sip of coffee.

"I ran through a bunch of possibilities when I first found it," he said, sitting down next to her. "That this *is* Harry. That he was Bo's son and they were estranged, maybe from when Harry was very young."

"Could be. He never said anything about his childhood. He never even talked about his mom, maybe because her death was too painful?"

She tried to remember if he'd *ever* talked about his mother, but nothing came to mind. Maybe he'd mentioned her a couple times in the most casual way. Like one time she'd asked, *Want to stop at Tony's Pizza?* And he'd said, *Sure, I love that place. I used to go with my mom as a kid.* And then she'd want to ask if he and his mom had been close, but something in his expression had always stopped her. Like she'd be prying.

She recalled thinking about that on the nights they weren't together, wondering why she always held back with him, since it wasn't really her way. *He was keeping you out, that's why*, she realized. He'd never allowed her to feel truly comfortable with him.

She bit her lip, wanting to shake these thoughts. *Get back to the conversation*, she told herself. "He never talked about her. And the two times I asked about his father had made it very clear he didn't want to talk about the man."

Harry's mood had changed for a good half hour after she'd asked about his dad. Just in the most general way too. But then he'd seemed to get over it, like he'd shuttered it back up again. So much for getting this out of her head. Then again, maybe it was good for her to talk about it. Maybe it helped in ways she didn't realize.

Gracie sipped her coffee, letting her gaze drift out the window at the evergreens. "Another time he said that thinking about the past only brought him down. Like he was telling me not to ask again. I remember him looking at me after that and adding that he was his own man, making his own way, and he liked focusing on the here and now."

She realized now that she hadn't been very comfortable with Harry. That there'd been a distance between them she couldn't breach. She'd been aware of that then, of course, but she'd chalked it up to dating just a couple of months. They'd seen each other a few times a week. So, maybe ten times total. And a lot of that time had been spent in bed. *Not* talking.

Harry had liked movies, same as her, and so they'd watched a lot of Netflix, take-out on the coffee table. Also not talking.

She hadn't really focused on that then either. The not talking.

Uneasy with her thoughts, the memories that she'd never really had a handle on, Gracie stood. She needed a moment. She glanced at West with something of a smile to let him know she was okay, and walked over to the playpen, which was just a few feet away from the table.

Liam was still happily sitting, now batting at the bunny and cooing.

Look what you missed, Harry Ahern, she thought. *For a good two and a half months, you could have seen this beautiful boy. Held him, known him. And you chose not to.* She mentally shook her head and turned.

"You okay, Gracie?" West asked.

His voice was like a soothing balm.

She came back to the table, the sight of West Calhoun making her feel better. She dropped down on the chair, wrapping both hands around the mug of coffee. "We've talked about how I've never been able to understand how a man who'd just heard he was going to be a father could just turn his back on his own baby."

West nodded, his warm blue eyes intent on her. He was such a good listener. She always had the sense that she had his full attention. And appreciated that, particularly now when she felt like hell.

She gave a small shrug. "But…maybe Harry's childhood had been hard and lonely, and the idea of his own family, having a child of his own, scared him to the point that he did just walk away. I don't know, West. Maybe I'm looking for excuses. Maybe for Harry Ahern, it was just out of sight, out of mind."

"Or maybe the knowledge that he had a baby out there was all he thought about," West said softly. "Maybe it haunted him."

She really didn't know. Because she clearly hadn't known Harry the way she'd thought she had. And that would always bother her.

"I thought I knew him." She added, "Well, as much as you could know someone you'd been dating two months. He really seemed true blue to me. He had a seriousness to him." She shook her head. But she hadn't known a thing about him other than the basics. "After he just disappeared on me, I really worried that my judgment was off. I know it's not and that people can just shock and surprise you for their own reasons, their own traumas." She bit her lip again and looked away. "You want to hear something crazy?"

"Yes," he said.

She looked at West then. This kind, thoughtful, wonderful man. Committed father. Committed rancher. *Committed*. That was the difference between Harry Ahern and West Calhoun.

West showed every day that commitment meant something to him. From the smallest thing of worrying that his daughter didn't wear a hat on a cold Wyoming winter morning to rushing out to pick Alexa up from a study party when it was clear something had gone wrong. The man *cared*. And he showed it all the time.

What had Harry cared about? She thought about that now. He'd cared about his job as a cowboy on a big local ranch. Showing up on time. Working late if he was needed. But he hadn't had family when Gracie dated him and so she'd never gotten to see him as a caring son or worried brother or a grandson going to help out his granddad with yardwork. No, she hadn't really known Harry at all. And he'd shown her who he was when he'd turned his back on her. She just hated that it was true. That he'd done that to her, to his baby.

West was waiting for her to continue, his gaze on her. And the more he looked at her with those caring, intelligent, always thinking eyes, the safer she felt with him.

"Even though I was so wrong about Harry," she finally said, "I do feel like I can trust *you*. Because of what I've seen and heard with my own eyes and ears. You're such a good man. Such a good father, West. But am I just a big trusting fool?"

"Gracie, I wish I could grab you into a hug because I really want to. To make you feel safe. And because I care about you. But because we're supposed to be hands-off, let me just tell you this. You *can* trust me. I promise you that. I'd never do anything that wasn't in your or Liam's best interests. I'll always take the two of you into consideration. In all regards."

Meaning the ranch—*and* personally.

"Which was why I was so quick to agree that we

should keep things to friendship," he added. "That way I won't break the promise I just made to you."

She managed a smile but she felt…all jumbled up. They did need to keep things platonic. But all she wanted right now *was* that hug from him. A big, warm hug, to be wrapped in those strong, trustworthy arms. And she couldn't go there with him.

So she nodded. "And then, that way, my faith in people will be restored, so all's good here."

Not quite, but it was a little something. She felt better than she had two minutes ago, that was for sure.

Her eyes went to the photo. She needed to change the subject—from them back to the mystery that had dropped into their lives. "How can we find out who this might be?" she asked, gesturing at it. "Who can we talk to from Bo's life? Someone who can shed some light on his past."

West studied her for a few seconds as if assessing if she was okay. He seemed satisfied that she was. "That's the thing. He wasn't close with anyone. Not the lawyer, who I'd never seen before the funeral and will-reading. No rancher buddies, though three local ranch owners with similar type operations did come to the funeral to pay respects. I think we should start where Bo lived *before* Bear Ridge. We could drive out and ask around about him. Be amateur detectives."

"I thought you tried to do an online search and nothing came up except links to Heartland Hollows and Bear Ridge?" she asked.

"Last night, after Alexa went to bed, the photo got me thinking. I did another online search for his name and Wyoming and the word *address*. It turned up one of those potentially scammer-type URLs listing addresses and phone numbers for people. The thumbnail noted a previous residence for Bo was in Brewer. Another search for the exact address was a ranch called Westwood Ranch—or it just might be called that now. It's something. And I think worth a trip out to Brewer."

"Let's do it," she said with a determined gleam in her eyes. "I think we have a good two hours we can leave the ranch in the staff's hands—between noon and two. And that would allow you home in time to meet Alexa's bus at three."

He nodded. "Perfect timing for us both. Hopefully we'll get our answers this afternoon."

And then maybe they could go back to focusing on being co-owners and things would settle down. But Gracie had a feeling that what was between them was just getting started.

Chapter Ten

At noon, West and Gracie arrived in Brewer, a sprawling town thirty minutes away with a vibrant downtown. He had a good feeling about this venture, that it would lead to something—if not the answer they were looking for, a step toward it.

As he looked around for a parking spot on Brewer Boulevard, he glanced at Gracie and could see the drive, even just the brief time away from the ranch and regular life—and their conversation—had done her good. She'd seemed so blue earlier in the kitchen, when she'd been talking about Harry and their relationship.

How he'd wanted to hold her again. The urge to get up and wrap his arms around her, bring her some comfort, had been so strong. But having a plan for a couple of hours away from Heartland Hollows definitely seemed to cheer her up some. Good.

The Dawsons were babysitting for the day and Alexa was in school, so the plan was to use these hours wisely. Gracie had done some research on Westwood Ranch, a cattle ranch in business the past ten years, which indicated that the owner had changed the name from when Bo had owned it. Then again, the online search he'd done had linked Bo to that ranch, so who knew anything? Maybe Bo had bought it as Westwood Ranch and kept it, and so had the new owners.

While West had driven, Gracie had tried to dig deeper into Westwood Ranch to see what it had been named before Bo had owned the property, but nothing came up. No matter, they had a good place to start and were here.

There were one-of-a-kind shops and restaurants on the main streets, and big-box stores off the highway. The sight of a cafeteria-style café where you ordered at the counter made him realize how hungry he was; he'd last had a cream-cheese slathered bagel and coffee at 5:00 a.m.

"Why don't we grab a quick lunch and make a plan for going over to the Westwood Ranch?" he asked. "I'm craving a turkey club and steak fries."

She nodded with a smile. "I am so in the mood for chicken salad on sourdough bread."

They headed inside JoJo's Great Eats Café, placed their orders and took their little number sign to a table by a window. Once they sat, West realized why he'd needed to take a break when stopping for lunch hadn't even been a thought. Something was on his mind.

"It's twelve fifteen," he said. "That's when Alexa's lunch period starts. She was worried about Riley and Lauren ignoring her today, how things would be."

"I was thinking about that, too, last night and this morning. It's gonna hurt, no way around that, but I think she went to school today feeling supported by her own feelings. I like that."

He instantly brightened. "That exactly what I told her yesterday. She's standing up for what's important to her. I do think that'll carry her."

She smiled that beautiful, warm, compassionate smile. He'd always been one to feel alone—to the point that it would propel him to think about getting back out there in the dating world. And since he'd lost Bo, his pillar, he'd been hit with that lack of support hard. But Gracie's smile, her kindness, her insightful wisdom, had changed that. Never more so than last night and right now.

How the hell was he going to turn off these feelings hitting him left and right? He looked out the window to escape her beautiful face for a moment. It was a cold day so not too many people were out and about, and there was some snow clinging to the trees in the park at the town green. When he turned his attention back to his lunch date, he could barely drag his eyes off her again.

Luckily, a waiter appeared with a tray holding their sandwiches and drinks.

They ate and talked about Brewer, which they'd both been to many times. Brewer was where everyone went when shopping local couldn't be an option. Plus there was a small rodeo that drew crowds every weekend, one of the reasons the downtown area had evolved into a fun destination.

"What do you think about driving out to the Westwood Ranch, knocking on the door, and asking if they recall the previous owner?" he said, dipping a fry in ketchup.

"I think it's our best bet. If that's a wash, we can go into the feedstores and any ranch-related businesses and ask around if anyone recalls Bo Bixby. Ten years isn't *that* long ago. Someone will remember him."

"And, hopefully, if he did have a child—a son."

She nodded and put down her sandwich half as if the whole subject made her uneasy.

He took a chance on asking what he was pretty sure was bothering her. "Gracie, does it feel like a lot to take in that Bo might be Liam's grandfather?"

She bit her lip. "Yeah. I can't really figure out why it has me feeling some kind of way. After all, I'd finally have answers. I'd know more about my son's family history." She glanced out the window then back at him. "But I guess what makes it hard is that Bo is *gone*. Just like Harry. Like, I finally might have found family for Liam on his dad's side, and he's gone."

Without thinking, he took her hand on the table and held it, and she allowed it, maybe needing that gesture of comfort as much as he thought she did.

"It's why if Bo does turn out to be Liam's grandfather," he said, "if we're on the right trail here—I love that Liam has inherited Heartland Hollows. That's special, Gracie."

She seemed to brighten. "It is. That's true."

"The ranch was Bo's pride and joy, what he put his heart and soul into because, for whatever reason, he couldn't put it into family. I don't know why that was. And again, maybe we're wrong about all this. But it's just feeling like the most reasonable explanation."

Gracie nodded. "You know, maybe Bo wasn't the

reclusive loner he'd become when he bought Heartland Hollows. If he was Harry's dad, maybe whatever happened with Harry's mom changed him."

"Yeah, maybe." He looked at their plates and realized they were done with lunch. He'd taken care of the bill at the counter, so they cleared the table and headed out.

"Well, at least I feel like we're close to getting somewhere," she said as they got back inside the SUV. "We'll go to Westwood Ranch. I'm ready to learn whatever the truth is."

He was about to press the start button but looked at her instead. "And whatever it is, however it makes you feel, just know that I'm here for you, Gracie."

She smiled at him. "I truly know that. I could not do this alone. Any of it."

He held her gaze for a moment, and then they were off, the map app on Gracie's phone providing directions.

They pulled into the drive for the ranch and the house came into view, white with black shutters and a wraparound porch, and a big red barn up the path where a couple of hands were at work. Westwood Ranch was a smaller version of Heartland Hollows, a herd grazing in the far pastures.

He and Gracie walked up the porch steps and before West could even lift a hand to knock, the door opened and a friendly-faced woman appeared. "You folks lost?"

West smiled. "No, we're actually wondering if

you knew the previous owner of this property—Bo Bixby?"

"Oh, yes, Bo," she said. "My husband and I bought the place from him as new ranchers. He was so good at all facets of the business that the transition to taking it over was so smooth."

West nodded. "I'm the foreman at the ranch he bought in Bear Ridge ten years ago. He was one of the best in the industry, for sure."

"Was?" she repeated, looking from West to Gracie.

Gracie explained that Bo had passed away a little over a week ago and that they'd inherited the Bear Ridge property from him. "We don't have much information on Bo on a personal level, and we're wondering if during the buying process he might have mentioned family, relatives, children?"

The woman thought for a second. "Hmm, it was a long time ago now and I don't recall him saying anything about himself that wasn't connected to the ranch. But I've never forgotten something about him."

He glanced at Gracie, whose eyes had widened at that tidbit. They both looked back to the woman.

"I asked if he'd raised kids on the ranch, since I was newly pregnant at the time," she said, "and planned on four or five kids running around, and was curious about the creek that ran through the property and the best tree for a tire swing, that kind of thing. Well, I tell you, his whole demeanor changed. For a moment he looked so crestfallen I wished I hadn't asked. I assumed maybe he'd lost a child," she added on something of a reverent whisper.

West took in a breath. *What happened, Bo?* he wondered, his heart going out to his friend and mentor up in heaven.

A phone rang inside the house and so they thanked the woman for her time. She smiled at them and went back inside.

Once they were heading down the drive, Gracie said, "Well, if Harry was Bo's son, he certainly was alive when Bo owned Westwood Ranch. That was ten years ago. Harry would have been nine years old."

West nodded. "If Bo had been 'crestfallen' at the question, that has to mean there was some conflict between Bo and Harry—or between Bo and Harry's mom, maybe. I just don't know."

"Let's go ask around town," she said. "A feedstore is probably a good second stop."

"I know where there's a big one," he said. "It's very popular."

In no time they were pulling open the door to Brewer's Feed and Supply. West spotted a man around Bo's age wearing the feedstore hat and pin on his shirt, and as he and Gracie approached, the guy, Ed, asked if he could be of help.

West introduced himself and Gracie as recent owners of a ranch in Bear Ridge that had belonged to Bo Bixby. "Did you know him, by any chance?"

"Oh, sure, I remember Bo," Ed said. "Came in several times a year with a couple of hands to explain what's what to them and buy a bunch of things. I know he sold the place that's now Westwood—must be at least ten years now."

West nodded. He figured he'd just ask outright like he had at the ranch. "I'm wondering if you know if he had any family. A wife, children?"

Ed thought for a moment. "Can't recall, honestly. Bo wasn't much of a socializer, I do remember that."

A few people were coming up to the counter with carts and baskets.

"When it rains, it pours," Ed said, moving over behind the register.

Gracie glanced at West then at Ed. He could see how disappointed she was. "Well, we appreciate your time."

Ed snapped his fingers. "You know who to ask, though—Petey Glovers. Yeah, old Petey. He keeps up on all the ranchers in town, then and now. He could tell you who owned what a hundred years ago. Petey was head of the association back then when Bo owned Westwood. But he's out of town visiting his daughter who just had another baby. I remember him saying he'd be back for the rodeo on Saturday. He's volunteering at the fundraising booth for the Brewer Rancher's Association. Tall, red hair. Can't miss him."

Red hair. One of the ranchers who West hadn't recognized at Bo's funeral had had red hair. And in fact, if West was remembering correctly, he hadn't come to the reception at the house. Maybe he'd had somewhere else to be.

West would have liked some information today, but at least they had what sounded like a great lead. "We'll look for him there, thanks, Ed."

As he and Gracie left the store, she said, "It's just a

couple of days. I can wait. Since, honestly, who knows what we might hear?"

West had an uneasy feeling they might hear something that would leave them both unsettled. For West, about the man he considered like a father figure the past ten years. And for Gracie, quite possibly her baby son's flesh and blood.

"Agreed," he said. "Head home?"

She nodded. "I miss Liam. And the ranch. It's beginning to feel more and more like home."

He was very glad to hear that. "Good," he said.

But a little voice inside him was thinking, *You're feeling more and more like home to me.*

Gracie's mom and grandmother had wanted to come see what Gracie had done with the house in the past days, so she called Linda Dawson when West had dropped her off to let her know she was home from Brewer. She had a good hour before she'd have to get to her Heartland Hollows To-Do List, all of which she could bring Liam along to in the chest carrier. She was so excited to see not only Liam but the warm, comforting, familiar faces of her family that she was waiting on the porch despite the picked-up wind. Her mom's car drove up and parked, and Gracie went to meet them.

Until she had Liam in her arms, reveling in the wonderful, sturdy weight of him, his big, curious blue eyes and giggles and babbles lifting her heart, she hadn't realized quite how unsettled she was about what she and West might learn about Bo's past.

Her son's past. Her son's *life*.

Once they were all in the house, her grandmother putting the pastries they'd gotten from the bakery on a plate on the table, her mom making coffee, and Gracie settling Liam into his high chair with a handful of Cheerios, Gracie caught them all up. Particularly on West finding the photo of the boy in Bo's desk—the only thing in any of the drawers—and the reason for their trip to Brewer.

Her mother gasped as she poured the coffee, adding cream and sugar the way they all liked. "So Liam could be Bo Bixby's grandson. It makes sense, so I have a good feeling it'll end up being the answer."

Her grandmother nodded. "Yes, I think so too. Everything adds up to that. The inheritance. The photo in the desk."

Gracie popped up to help bring over the mugs. Once they were all seated, Gracie realized her grandmother was staring at her—with narrowed eyes and a slightly amused, curious expression.

Dorothea cut a lemon Danish in two and put it on her plate. "You and West sure have been spending time together."

Two sets of green Dawson eyes looked at her expectantly.

Do not tell them about the kiss. Because then you'll have to tell them about the plan to keep things between you two strictly professional.

And who could disagree with that? Huh, maybe she should tell them. So they'd hammer the point home.

That getting involved with West could mean trouble down the line. And not just for her heart. For her child.

"Okay, I kissed West," she blurted out, desperately needing to say it aloud—and get their takes on the situation.

Her grandmother paused with a piece of Danish halfway to her mouth. "What kind of kiss? A quick peck?"

"A *movie* kiss," Gracie said.

A very pleased smile lit up her mother's face. "And so you're a couple now? Clearly, traipsing off to Brewer to do some sleuthing, stopping for lunch…"

"Hardly, actually," she said, and realized just how wistful she felt about how things were between her and West. "We can't get romantically involved—and we're both in agreement on that. If something goes wrong with us and we end up bitter and angry at each other, the ranch suffers. *Liam* suffers. I was tasked to manage his inheritance until he's twenty-one. Kissing the co-owner isn't the way to do that."

"Why would you end up bitter and angry at each other?" her mother asked.

"Because romances usually end," Gracie explained. "And end badly."

Her mother and grandmother looked at each other, then at Gracie.

"Honey," her gram said, "your parents have been happily married for thirty-one years. I was happily married for fifty-two years. Why aren't we your model? Why aren't we your yardstick?"

Good question. But Gracie had an answer.

"Your marriages *would* be," she said. "And should

be. But every relationship *I've* had hasn't worked out. I told my baby's father I was pregnant and he left town to avoid me and fatherhood. I was absolutely bitter and angry. That's what happens when people disappoint you so profoundly."

"And West Calhoun is going to profoundly disappoint you?" her mother interjected as she broke a scone in two. "He sounds like a godsend to me."

"He is," Gracie said before she could stop herself. "He's really great."

"There you have it!" Linda Dawson said.

"You make such a beautiful couple," her grandmother put in. She put her hands up in a square as if she was seeing a photo of the two of them.

Grace was shaking her head. "Even if we did start dating, I think West is looking for...something more practical. Not love and passion and happily-ever-after. He needs a solid stepmother for his daughter. Someone warm and wonderful and who can step into their busy lives."

"*You're* warm and wonderful," her grandmother said. "You'd make a great stepmom to a twelve-year-old."

"And besides," Linda Dawson put in, "aren't you looking for a warm and wonderful *responsible* father for Liam?"

Gracie froze for a second. Huh. They were actually looking for the same thing.

Except West didn't want to be in love with his future wife. He wanted something...practical. Something lasting. Beautiful in a different way.

And Gracie...what did she want?

Love. Real love, the passionate kind, the abiding kind, the kind that lasted through thick and thin.

How did she still believe in it? She had no idea how, but she did. She wanted it all.

But the whole thing was moot. She and West were going to be friends only. Keep their relationship professional.

"I just know that we're not dating," she said. "And that we're not going to date. We're friends. Partners. As we should be—for the sake of the ranch and Liam's inheritance." Gracie gave a nod and then sipped her coffee. Making assertions about her and West's relationship, absolutes, helped her feel less off balance.

She caught the sly smile her mom and grandmother sent each other. Gracie could read it loud and clear. *Oh, right, try to get in love's way.*

She froze at the word *love*. No one had said anything about love. She wasn't falling in love with the man—it was way too soon. Wasn't it?

Could she fall in love without her say-so? Could it happen slowly right under her nose?

Sometimes it seemed that way. When she looked at West and couldn't bear to even glance away from that face, from all that was in his eyes. When he sneaked in a hand squeeze, a hug just when she needed strong arms around her. And that kiss... As if she could ever forget how *that* had felt.

"Oh, Mom, we have to run," Linda Dawson said, "the indoor shuffleboard tournament starts in a half hour at the rec center."

They packed up, leaving the pastries, which Gracie

appreciated. She scooped her up her son, and his grandmother and great-grandmother both gave him big kisses on the cheek. Gracie then settled Liam into his playpen.

As the three of them walked to the door, her grandmother took her hand. "Honey, just promise me you'll let things take their course."

"Promise me, too," her mother said, zipping up her pea coat and wrapping her scarf around her neck. "For once, I'm happy to have you just jump in. I like West Calhoun for you."

"Same," Dorothea said with a firm nod.

Gracie helped her grandmother on with her long down coat. *Let things take their course.* That would mean going with the flow. With their feelings. Their attraction...

Things could move fast.

Like into bed.

"Just don't try to control what can't be controlled," Dorothea added. "Not everything ends in disaster. Just look at me and your parents. At your mother's oldest and dearest friend Carlene. So many happy marriages."

True, Gracie thought. All true. But the divorce rate *was* pretty high, wasn't it?

Her mom narrowed her eyes at Gracie, clearly realizing where her thought had taken her. "A solid relationship takes finding your person—and then making it work. If you don't want the relationship to end in bitterness and anger, then make sure it *doesn't*. Make sure you two hear each other, compromise, listen."

Oh, just that? Gracie smiled and wrapped her arms around her beloved grandmother, then hugged her mother. "Anyway, he and I are on the same page. We're friends."

"Sure," her grandmother singsonged with a twinkle in her eye. "Whatever you say, honey."

Her mother laughed as they pulled her into another round of warm hugs and she walked them out, watching until they drove away. She wanted them back immediately.

She wanted to feel as sure as they seemed to that not only were she and West meant to be, but that all would work out. No disaster. The inheritance secure. The ranch just fine.

She sighed.

Inside the house, she was about to scoop Liam from his playpen, but he'd fallen asleep.

She stared down at her beautiful baby son, his little nose, his adorable big cheeks. She never saw Harry in his features; Liam was her mini me, from the coloring to even his expression.

Stop thinking about Harry and the past. She knew what her relatives were saying was right and true. There were good, lasting relationships out there. Long, loving marriages. Her family *was* proof of that.

But she could try to make things work with West and it was possible that the relationship would fail anyway. That was the problem. The failure. Because of how much damage it could do.

Stop it, she told herself. *You two decided to be platonic for good reason. So just let it be.*

Move on.

She tried to clear her head from thoughts of West,

thoughts of Harry—anything connected to her love life, past and present. *Look for Bo Bixby's features in Liam's face.* She'd tried that before, based on photos of the man, but except for the blue eyes, he looked as much like Bo as she did. She peered down at Liam, but given that his eyes were closed, now wasn't the time to study him for a family resemblance.

Her phone rang just she needed a break from herself. West.

"Hi," she said. "I'm glad you called. I've been wondering if you'd heard from Alexa today. I hope she's doing okay with all that happened with her friends—or former friends."

"She texted me from her school tablet that Riley and Lauren gave her the cold shoulder all morning and that she tried to find her version of your lab partner, whatever that means."

Gracie smiled. "It's a good thing. And very sweet."

"Actually, Alexa is the reason I called."

Gracie's stomach tightened. She cared about that girl—and braced herself for hearing about anything that hurt Alexa.

"I got an email from Bear Ridge Middle School," West said. "A flyer and form asking for volunteers to chaperone the dance on Saturday night. I'm in and was wondering if you'd be up for that too? I have no doubt she'll ask me to ask you. But please feel absolutely free to say you can't."

Oh, phew, she thought with a relieved smile.

"I've love to," she said. "And I'm sure I'll be approved since I volunteer in the Bear Ridge school system—if a teacher needs some help in the classroom, whether with reluctant readers or helping high schoolers craft essays. I'm happy to be there for her."

"That will mean a lot to her. Thank you. That means Saturday will be busy for both of us—going back to Brewer to talk to Petey at his rodeo booth about Bo, and then chaperoning the dance at night."

She swallowed at that last thing he'd said.

They'd be dancing too.

Chest to chest for slow dances, his arm around her, hers on his shoulders if not around his neck.

Kissing distance for at least two or three minutes per song. That was a long time to be that close to someone who made your knees weak.

Goose bumps skittered up her spine at just the thought of him holding her close.

Slow dancing for a few hours to whatever Generation Y was listening to these days would make her mom and grandmother's wishes come true. Would make Gracie's fantasies come true.

But *passion like that* tended to burn out just as quickly as it ignited.

There might be hurt feelings or dashed expectations and one or both would get hurt. A small argument would fester. Turn into something big.

And both their fears would be realized. Everything they were trying to avoid with the deal to keep their relationship professional would blow up in their faces.

Do not *slow dance with the man. Stick to that mantra and you'll be fine.*

Chapter Eleven

Ever since Gracie had agreed to chaperone with him, all of a half hour ago, West could not stop thinking about the two of them slow dancing. He'd just have to avoid that and stick to the sidelines, doing their chaperoning duties, like watching for any misbehaving seventh graders.

As he was heading from the barn to his cabin, Jackie the cat trailing him, his phone rang. Alexa. He crossed his fingers that she wasn't calling him because she was sobbing.

"Hi, Dad, guess what? I was invited to my new friend Alana's house after school to study for Friday's math quiz. Can I go? She said I could stay for dinner too."

Relief. "Sure. What time should I pick you up?"

"She said seven thirty would be good. Can you believe that I actually have a new friend? Tell Gracie she was right!" She gave him the address—the house was just five minutes from the ranch.

West smiled. "I definitely will. See you later."

"Oh, wait—Dad? Forms were sent to parents about chaperoning the dance. Can you *and* Gracie chaperone? Please, Dad? Will you ask her?"

He'd called that one. It would help to have her support system there in a school-requested capacity. "I absolutely will. I'm sure Gracie will too."

"Yay," she said.

They disconnected and he texted Gracie.

Alexa just called to say she was invited to her new friend's house to study for a math quiz—and to tell you you were right. She also asked if we'd sign up to be chaperones at the dance.

He smiled again at her response.

You definitely called *that*. I'm so happy she made a new friend.

Me too. Now that I unexpectedly have the next few hours free, I thought I'd do some digging into Harry Ahern's background and see what I could find. You okay with that? Maybe I'll find some definite link between him and Bo as father and son. Just in case Saturday afternoon is a bust.

I'm okay with it. Let me know if you find anything. I don't know if you'll have luck, though. I did an online search on Harry when he first disappeared on me, and nothing came up at all. There are several Harry Aherns in Wyoming, apparently.

It might lead nowhere. But you never know. I'll call you if anything pops up.

When they disconnected, West got right to work at his laptop on the sofa. He figured he'd start with the basics. Harry Ahern. Brewer, Wyoming. He recalled Gracie saying that was where he was from.

Nothing.

Harry Ahern. Wyoming. There weren't all that many and none seemed the right age. A little further digging brought up a previous address—in a small town bordering Brewer called Windy Hill. Entering Harry Ahern and Windy Hill in the search bar didn't get him anywhere. Except, what was this? Another previous address in Windy Hill for Leticia Ahern and Harrison Ahern. So, his full name was Harrison.

He did a search for Leticia Ahern. A short obituary popped up.

Leticia Ahern, devoted mother of 18-year-old Harrison, passed peacefully in her sleep after a short illness. She was 40 years old. Raised in foster care, Ms. Ahern had no family other than her beloved son, and a few treasured friends. A private memorial service will be held in Windy Hill.

The obituary was dated eleven years ago.

West shouldn't read too much from a four-line obituary, but he got the sense Harry had been nurtured by a loving mother. But there was no mention of an ex-husband or current husband, any mention of who Harry's father was. No link to Bo Bixby, or an obvious link, but that didn't mean Letitia Ahern and Bo hadn't crossed paths—and been romantically involved.

West wished those few treasured friends had been named so that he could reach out to them, but with a private memorial, finding out any details of where it had been held and who'd attended wouldn't be simple.

His best bet for information just might be with Petey Glovers from the rancher's association. West had gotten the impression he was an old-timer with an excellent memory, particularly when it came to area ranchers.

He picked up his phone and called Gracie.

"Everything okay?" she asked. "No calls from Alexa to come get her from her study plans with her new friend?"

He smiled. "Thankfully, no. I wanted to tell you that I did find something about Harry—his mother." He read her the short obituary.

"Oh," Gracie said. "I like the beloved part. It sounds like they were close, right?"

"That's the sense I got too."

"She died in July—eleven years ago. That would have been just a month after he graduated from high school. Almost like she hung on for that." She let out a breath. He waited for her to continue, but she didn't.

"Gracie? You okay?"

She didn't respond for a few seconds. "That's Liam's other grandmother. I didn't know her name or anything about her before. Letitia Ahern. Beloved mother..."

He could tell that Gracie was crying. And seemed to be trying to keep that from him. "I'm coming over, Gracie. Be there in two minutes."

"'K," she whispered.

He disconnected, which he hated doing, pulled on

his leather jacket and hurried out, jogging the quarter mile to the ranch house. He knocked, and she opened, tears in her eyes, her expression sad and heavy. He wrapped his arms around her and used his foot to push the door closed.

He stepped back a bit, and wiped away her tears. She exhaled and took his hand and led him over to the sofa, dropping down. He sat beside her. He could see Liam napping in the playpen by the patio doors.

She followed his gaze. "Good thing he needed an extra nap because I wouldn't want him to see me all teary and flustered." She took in a breath, her eyes misting again. She stared at their hands, still entwined. Neither let go.

"I guess I'm just emotional. I keep thinking about all the *losses*. Harry abandoning me. Then dying so young. Not having anyone to contact on his side, no one to share the loss with or the news of the baby with his relatives or friends. And worse, that my son would never know his father. Or his paternal grandmother or grandfather. Two weeks ago, Liam had another grandfather right here in town—I truly believe Bo was his grandpa. And he was right here. Ten minutes away from my house."

"I get it," he said gently, resting his head atop hers. He could tell she was upset, very emotional, and he didn't want to rush at her with words, trying to somehow make this better for her. It hurt.

"And that obituary," she said, sniffling again. "A mother raised in foster care with no family. No mention of a husband left behind along with her son. Harry was all alone in the world. And he still walked away from me—and his baby to be. How? How does someone do that?" Her voice was barely a whisper and cracking, and he tightened his arm around her. "I know I keep asking that, but how, West? *How?*"

"I really don't understand it myself. It's hard to fathom." As a widower who'd lost his wife, a father whose daughter had lost her mother at two years old, someone—especially so alone—walking away from the gift of family... *How?* was right.

She took in a breath. "Maybe some form of self-protection? Like I thought before."

"Maybe," he said. But what he was thinking—and would never say *ever*—was that he thought it had been cowardly. *Step up, man.*

But he had no right to judge.

She sat back a little and rested her head against his shoulder, her hand still in his. "When I heard that he died and I had no one to reach out to, I was so upset. Finally, my mom and grandmother sat me down and told me they knew it hurt, but that my infant son needed me to be a strong and joyful mother. That helped me so much. I completely changed my focus."

The ole paradigm shift. He could just picture the warm, nurturing pair rallying to Gracie's side, supporting her, being there for her. He was so glad she had them in her life.

"I just had to accept that Liam would have a very small family—just us. And we're a small bunch, as it is. My dad reminded me it's about *quality* not quantity." She smiled, though her chin was a bit wobbly. "He assured me not to worry, that his grandson would have a loving, doting family who'd annoy him to no end."

West smiled. "Your dad is awesome. But I do understand why you were sad, Gracie. It bothered me a lot that there was no one there for Bo. Yeah, a few people came to the funeral to pay their respects. But in those last weeks, last days, *no one* came to the house to see him, sit with him, talk with him for a bit. He was alone in the world except for me. And you know, I said something about that to Alexa one day when I was really down. And she said, 'Yeah, Dad, but you're *a lot*.'" He smiled. "God, did that make me laugh. And feel better." His own paradigm shift. Out of the mouth of a tween.

Gracie nodded and sniffled, a smile finally forming on her pretty face. "I love that, West. She was saying you might have been just one person, but your love is mighty. And big. And plentiful. How beautiful."

Huh. He felt his heart expand in his chest, getting bigger like the Grinch's did in that old animated holiday TV show.

She looked up him, her expression brightening. "I'm going to look at Liam's small family of just us that way too. Mighty and big and plentiful." She sat up and looked at him, clasping his hand even tighter. "Thank you for coming over. For being here. You're always just what I need," she whispered.

She held his gaze, and he couldn't look away.

And then he kissed her.

Softly, holding the sides of her face in his hands, pulling away just an inch to make sure she was okay with that.

She let him know just *how* okay by pressing her soft lips back to his and wrapping her arms around his neck. He couldn't stop kissing her if he tried very hard. And he didn't want to stop.

He picked her up, her expression going from surprise to sultry. She kissed him as he carried her up the stairs to her bedroom, her long blond hair hanging down. He was dimly aware of the baby monitor on her bedside table as he neared the bed. They'd hear Liam if he chose this most inopportune of times to wake up.

West barely put her down on the bed before she was on her knees before him, unbuttoning his shirt. Unzipping his jeans.

He could feel his erection straining against his boxer briefs. And when a soft, cool hand slipped under the waistband and down until she held him tightly, she groaned. He had her sweater off and liked how easily he could peel down her leggings.

Now she was only in her bra and underwear, a silky pale pink color. The deep cleavage of lush breasts had him unable to wait another second to unhook the bra and feel her creamy fullness, then take one rosy nipple into his mouth.

She threw her head back and moaned, which had him even harder—something he hadn't thought possible.

With a finger, he inched down her underwear, and she did the same with his.

Naked.

"I want you so bad," he whispered. That was all he could think about.

"Same for me," she whispered back.

And then he was inside her, rocking, pulsating, trailing kisses along her neck, her collarbone. For the first time in a very long time, he felt every sensation, every emotion—not just the intensity of sex, but all he felt for this beautiful, wonderful woman.

Her nails were digging into his back as she neared climax and when she finally did, trying not to scream with a sexy fist in her mouth, he finally let go himself.

She curled up next to him, her head on his chest, his arm around her.

"Amazing," she said.

"Amazing," he agreed.

There was no need to say anything more. They weren't supposed to be here, based on their own *previous* agreement, which would not have included *amazing* sex, let alone a second kiss.

Right now, they were here, and where this would lead, he didn't know. He just knew he wasn't moving a muscle.

Gracie had been in such a state of sated bliss that she hadn't felt a hint of worry in the fifteen minutes that she lay at West's side. She'd moved her head off his chest and they were facing each other, neither of them saying a word.

What was there to say? We shouldn't have done that? They'd done it.

Now what? was the question. But she wasn't going to bring that up. She had no idea how she felt about what this would mean. Neither of them was comfortable with the idea of a romantic relationship. But they were in the middle of one—clearly.

And to cling to this idea of a platonic relationship was futile, given that they'd just made love.

"I'm not sure what this means, West," she blurted out. "I'm nervous. What if this, what if that, and suddenly we're at each other's throats and you're trying to buy me out. Buy Liam out." She bit her lip. Why had she said all that?

He reached a hand to her cheek. "Gracie, all I know is that there's something very special between us. I think the only thing we can do is go with that. We're both going to be very mindful of protecting the ranch at all costs."

"Nothing ever works out," she whispered.

"Until it does," he said with a gentle smile, his blue eyes tender on her.

She wanted this. Her heart yearned for it. And to have this "warm, wonderful responsible man," to quote her mother, in Liam's life, from the age of six months...

Her toes were actually tingling with the excitement of it all—how strongly she felt for West Calhoun. That they'd just made love—and had serious chemistry in bed too. That he'd just said something so reassuring and promising.

Until it does...

She could hold on to that and stop being so scared of loving someone again.

"I do not want to leave this bed or your side, but it's seven forty-five and I need to pick up Alexa," he said, running a hand slowly down her hair and playing with the ends.

Maybe a good thing so she didn't spontaneously combust.

"That'll give us both time to think," she said with a soft smile.

"I'm trying *not* to think—overthink, Gracie. We can't force ourselves to back off when there's something so special here. I can't. And don't want to. We're both committed, caring people. And that's all we need to know right now. This is a real second chance at what we've both been missing out on."

"Well, when you put it like that," she said, leaning over to kiss him. "We'll take it slow and easy, right?"

"Slow and easy," he repeated, kissing her back and then getting out of bed. "I'm in."

"Me, too," she said, her heart practically bursting.

She watched him get dressed, fully enjoying every second of it.

And then after one more kiss, and a sweet look into her eyes, he was gone.

Sometimes good people said things in the moment that they absolutely meant. But then this or that happened and they suddenly didn't mean it later. That was what she was afraid of.

But right now, she was going to just lie here with her eyes closed and revel in how good she felt, how full, in her heart, in her head.

Chapter Twelve

"And guess what else about Alana," Alexa said as she sat at her desk and got her backpack ready for school tomorrow.

From the moment West had picked her up from her new friend's house, she'd been full of happy chatter about how well she and Alana had studied together, how nice her parents were, and that Alana also loved spaghetti tacos, just like Alexa and West did.

She hadn't said a word about her former friends, Riley and Lauren, and how they'd ignored her today. West had no doubt it had hurt and would sting for a while, but Alexa was excited about her new friendship and West was thrilled for his daughter.

"What?" West asked. "Wait, let me guess—she also loves scary movies like we do."

"Actually I don't know if she does. But probably!" She grinned. "Ready for it? She loves *gargoyles*!" She giggled and picked up the small statue she'd taken from the console table in the ranch house before Gracie had moved in. "I'm gonna take a photo with the iPad and show Alana. She'll love it. Maybe she'll help me name him. I haven't come up with the perfect name for him."

West smiled as she turned the gargoyle every which way to study him.

"Oh, wow," she said as a piece on the back of the statue slid down. "Did I break it?"

West stepped closer and looked. "Actually, I think it's a removable piece with a hollow area to store something, maybe." The piece slid right out of narrow grooves. "And is that something inside?" It was small, square and black, like a thick piece of paper.

Alexa carefully took it out. "It's a photo! Like one of those instant kinds they had when your grandma and grandma were young."

West stared at the photo—and could not help gasping. His heart started beating *fast*.

Why on earth would *this* have been tucked inside that statue that had been on Bo's console table? For safekeeping? To have it, yet hide it away? And right there by the front door so Bo was aware of it when he came in and left? But couldn't *see* it?

It was a photo of a gravesite with a headstone: *Harrison Ahern*.

Underneath, the dates he was born and died. Twenty-nine years apart.

And a line below.

Always in my heart.

There was no doubt now in West's mind. Harry Ahern was Bo's son. Immediately, twenty questions filled his head. All with no answers.

Alexa was looking from the photo to him and back again. "Dad? Who's Harrison Ahern? Did you know him?"

"I didn't know him. But Gracie did. I'd like to go show her this. You okay on your own for an hour?"

Alexa raised an eyebrow. "Of course. I'm *twelve*. I'll take pictures of the gargoyle while you're gone."

"Don't open the door for anyone, okay?"

"I know, I know," she said, her attention back on the statue.

He hurried out with the photo in his hand, opting to drive the minute to the ranch house to show her the photo as quickly as possible.

Not just because it connected Liam to Bo—finally.

But because it might give Gracie some peace. She hadn't seen Liam's father from the day she'd told him she was pregnant with his child. And then she'd learned he'd died.

That there had been a proper burial, a final resting place, would be meaningful to her.

And to have texted her the photo to talk about it that way wasn't going to cut it. If Gracie needed him, he wanted to be there for her.

When he pulled up at the house, he texted her to let her know he had something to show her. He was barely out of his pickup when she opened the door, crossing her arms against the cold, December night air.

Once they were inside, he showed her the photo and explained that Alexa had found it in a gargoyle statue she'd taken from the console table because she hadn't thought Gracie would want to see it every time she came in or out.

She stared at the photo, then slowly dropped down on the sofa. "I saw the obituary in the *Gazette*. It's how

I knew Harry died. It was very brief—'Harry Ahern, of Brewer, Wyoming, was killed recently in a motorcycle accident. He will be missed.' I even called the *Brewer County Gazette* to try to find out who'd submitted the obituary, but I was told it was dropped off anonymously in the mail slot. I'd been hoping to connect with that person, learn more about Harry. But that didn't happen."

She studied the photo, then got up and walked over to the sliding-glass doors to the deck, looking out at the night.

"You okay?" he asked, staying put on the couch. He wanted to give her whatever time she needed to digest this.

She turned and nodded. "If Bo had this photo, he must have gone to the funeral, right? If there was one. Or maybe he just arranged for the burial and headstone." She paused, tilting her head. "Bo knew about me and Liam—I wonder why he wouldn't have gotten in touch to tell me about the funeral."

"Good question. Unless he thought you knew about it? And how would Bo have known about you in the first place unless *Harry* told him about you and the baby. I guess Harry was keeping track of you—he knew you'd given birth."

"My parents did put a baby announcement in the paper—but in the *Bear Ridge Free Weekly*, not Brewer, where Harry lived. I wonder if Harry happened to see it? Maybe he was looking for an announcement around the time he figured I'd be due." She threw up her hands, her expression turning sad. "I don't know.

It's hard to imagine he'd keep tabs without even checking on me once."

He wanted to go over to her and hold her, but he knew he needed to let her have this moment, to digest and process. "Harry was a mystery. Just like Bo."

She nodded. "Like father, like son, perhaps."

She sat back down beside him, looking at the photo again. "I guess this must be somewhere in Brewer. I can call the cemeteries and find out which one. It means a lot to have a physical place where Liam can go when he's older."

West took her hand. "Absolutely."

She squeezed his hand and held on to it.

"Thanks for coming over with it," she said. "I'm glad to know he had a proper burial. He'd always said he was a loner and didn't have any close friends, just acquaintances. So I think it must have been Bo who'd arranged for the burial and the headstone."

"Sounds like it."

"Hopefully, Saturday, we'll get more info from the rancher association gentleman," she said. "Maybe all the pieces of the puzzle will finally fit in place."

He nodded and the moment she disengaged their hands, he missed the connection. "I wish I could stay for a while. But I should get back to Alexa. She had a great time at her new friend's house. They're both gargoyle fans."

Gracie smiled, her beautiful face lighting up. "I'm looking forward to the school dance. I'm glad to be a part of it. Glad we can dance all we want, cheek to cheek."

He smiled. "Same here."

As she walked him to the door, he thought of how they *would* be dancing cheek to cheek, chest to chest, and that it would likely lead to another magical experience between them. They were taking it slow, which was the best way to go.

But he couldn't wait to have her in his arms again.

After checking on Liam, who was still napping, Gracie flopped on her bed and FaceTimed Miranda. She filled her in on everything that had happened. Including tonight's revelations.

"Whoa. Wait a minute. I'm still on that you and West slept together."

Gracie thought about how natural it had felt. How emotional. All that had been building between them had culminated in the moment they'd kissed on the sofa, in the moment he'd picked her up and carried her to her bedroom.

"I love that he's always there for you," Miranda said. "That he rushed over with the photograph of the gravesite. Someone else might have texted it to you. Someone else might have let you see that when you were all alone with your baby—Harry's baby."

Gracie nodded. Exactly. She could count on West. She couldn't imagine him ever letting her down. He made that crystal clear with each day.

"I also love you two aren't going to try to force yourself to keep your hands and lips off," her friend added on a laugh. "That ship has definitely sailed."

"Very smooth sailing, at that," Gracie said with a grin.

Miranda laughed. "I can see in your face how happy you are. This is so great."

Gracie smiled. "We're definitely going to take it slow—which luckily has to be the case since we've both got kids. I can't just drop everything for a date and neither can he."

"I've been meaning to ask—what's his daughter like?"

Gracie pictured Alexa Calhoun, bursting with being twelve and all it wrought. Puberty. Crushes. Dances. "A total sweetheart. We've really connected."

"And West is literally partners with your six-month-old. Sounds very cozy all around!"

Gracie laughed. "I'm going to dare hope, Miranda. I'm in—all in. I like this man so, so much."

In fact, I'm falling in love... Those were words she was a little too nervous about to say aloud, to admit to herself. If she gave herself permission to go to those depths, she was afraid she'd lose control of her heart entirely.

"It's normal to be a little scared, though, right?" she asked.

"Of course. There are *two* of you. Separate people. But from everything you've shared with me, this is the man to risk all those scary lovey-dovey feelings for."

Exactly what Gracie thought.

"And I love that your next date is a middle school dance," Miranda added. "Family affair for sure. And speaking of, so the big mystery is solved? Liam is Bo Bixby's grandson and that's why Bo left him half the ranch?"

Family. It was so hard to apply the word to Bo and Harry.

"All the clues from Bo's side—Liam's inheritance, the two photographs, one of a young boy, one of Harry's headstone—sure point to that. It's just hard to understand when both Bo and Harry said they had *no* family. If they were father and son, that's exactly what they were. So what the hell? I don't get it."

"Sounds to me like there was some terrible reason for an estrangement."

A shiver ran up Gracie's spine. The idea of it was just so awful. What could have happened to cause the separation? And if that was the case, it raised a lot of questions. "Yeah, I'm thinking so too. I just wonder, then, how Bo knew about Liam at all. His birthdate. My name. He had the details of the birth."

"Oh, right," Miranda said. "Harry died just a few months after Harry was born. Maybe he told Bo during that time. Maybe they were estranged but started talking again?"

Gracie bit her lip and thought about that. "I just don't know. If they were talking again, why would Bo have said in the period after Harry's death that he had no family?"

Miranda sighed. "I know. Nothing about this adds up. It never did from the very beginning—the reading of the will. But Bo Bixby did leave your baby son half his ranch. Bo did have a photo of a little boy in his desk. A photo of Harry Ahern's headstone in that weird statue that used to be in the ranch house."

"You know what the saddest part of all this is to

me? That both Bo and Harry were alive when Liam was born. Liam's father. Liam's grandfather. He had them both—at a distance, yes. But he had them. And then, poof, they're both gone."

Miranda sucked in a breath and shook her head. "I know, honey. It's a lot to take in. And you're going to Brewer tomorrow to get answers—I really hope it works out."

"Me too." Gracie shook her own head to clear it. "Enough about all this—tell me all about your yoga teacher training and how the retreat's going."

Gracie relaxed as her friend told her funny stories, including a goat-yoga experience, and all her questions, all the speculation about her own life faded away.

"So are you actually looking forward to chaperoning the middle school dance?" Miranda said. "All those hormonal tweens?" She mock-shivered.

Gracie laughed. "I can't wait. Yesterday, I was worried a possible slow dance would make me unable to resist him. Now, we can slow dance all we want. Green light." With a yellow light very subtly flashing to be smart. She'd been hurt very badly before and, like Miranda had said, *she and West were two separate people*. She couldn't control what he felt or thought or did.

Her happiness over her new relationship with West was just too big to be squashed by nerves.

"I love this," Miranda said with a smile. "This is huge for *me*. Knowing that there really are second chances—you just have to be willing to take them when they come along. And when they feel right like this does."

Gracie nodded. "Absolutely. I'm definitely scared, though. It's so hard to believe I can really have this. That I won't get clobbered, you know?"

"Aww, Gracie, I totally understand. I just got divorced. Trust me, that I know how hard it must be to let yourself actually have this, to believe in it. But I'm so glad you are putting yourself out there, taking this chance. Because that means you're a true believer."

"In what?" Gracie asked.

"Love, silly. And thank God for Liam you are."

She'd found out that just yesterday. That she did still believe in love. With every day that West had been in her life, those little holes in her heart had been filling up.

"I feel better," Gracie said. "Thank you for everything."

"Any time. I want all the details next week. I've gotta run—literally—for our mandatory jog session. Love you, bye!"

Gracie disconnected with a smile and lay back on her bed, heart full, head clear.

But she sat up with a sudden awareness.

She loved West.

Chapter Thirteen

As West found a parking spot in the very crowded lot for the Brewer Holiday Rodeo on Saturday morning, he realized he and Gracie had spent the past forty minutes talking about everything but themselves and the photograph found in that gargoyle. Gracie had kept up a steady stream of conversation about old school dances and differences between their generation and Alexa's. He'd recognized within five minutes that she'd needed to keep her worries at bay, and so he, too, had kept the conversation light.

As they headed toward the ticket windows, he turned to Gracie and said, "I just want to say that if you hear something hard, I'm here for you, okay?"

"I know and I appreciate it. And really, West, same here. I know how you felt about Bo. That you came to think of him as like a father. I don't want you to hear anything that may—"

"Sting," he offered.

"Exactly."

He held out his arm and she smiled as she wrapped hers around it. They were dressed for the occasion, both in cowboy hats, Gracie's a light brown and his a dark brown. They both wore leather coats and jeans and cowboy boots. The littlest rancher in Wyoming, Liam Dawson, would be dressed the same but he was back in Bear Ridge with his doting grandparents and great-grandmother.

"Tickets are on me," he said.

"Then lunch is on me. If I can eat anything later."

"Deal," he said.

They passed various booths in the crowded event center, from food stalls to merchandise, lots of cowboy hats and boots. Finally, smack in the middle, was a booth with a sign reading Brewer Rancher's Association. And a banner below: Fundraiser. A dollar donation got you a pen with the association logo. A ten-dollar donation you got a T-shirt. A blown-up photo showed the various colors and sizes.

Two men sat on folding chairs in the booth—one in his forties, one in his seventies—and tall with red hair, as Ed at the feedstore had described Petey Glovers. West had definitely seen the man at Bo's funeral. He hadn't come to the reception at the house, though.

West said he'd like to buy four shirts; a navy men's large for himself, and then asked Gracie to pick out ones for herself, Alexa and a baby-sized one for Liam.

"Adorable," Grace said, looking at the photo, which included a baby in an orange T-shirt and a cowboy hat. "I'll also take one baby size in six-to-twelve months in orange, a woman's medium in blue and woman's small in purple."

West actually felt his heart move in his chest at that last one. He gave her hand a squeeze and wanted to pull her into his arms and hold her. "You're very thoughtful."

She squeezed his hand back.

There were no other people waiting at the booth, so it was a good time to talk to Petey.

He looked at the older man. "I was told that a Petey Glovers might be able to help us out with some information about someone who used to own a ranch in Brewer. Bo Bixby?"

"Ah, Bo. Lived and breathed ranching. I was sorry to hear he passed. I paid my respects at the funeral."

West nodded. "I recall seeing you there." Once again, West wondered if there was a reason Petey hadn't joined them at the reception. West had certainly never seen Petey before or after the funeral.

"You're the foreman of the Heartland Hollows, right?" Petey asked. "I remember seeing you there too. You had a real nice speech."

West hadn't been sure he'd get through the speech without breaking down. In less than two minutes, he'd spoken mostly of Bo's skills as a rancher and a businessman, but at the end, he'd added that Bo Bixby had been more than just a mentor for ten years, that he'd been a true friend. He'd gone back and forth about saying something about how Bo had felt like a father figure to him, but only because he didn't think Bo would like that, given how prickly he'd been. The word *friend* would mean a lot to Bo, and so West had gone with that.

He'd been the only person to speak at the funeral.

West nodded. "I'd worked for Bo for ten years, the last five as foreman. We were close."

Petey raised an eyebrow. "Bo, close to someone? I'm glad to hear it. When I knew Bo, he might as well have had a sign on him reading Stay Back Twenty Feet At All Times, In All Directions."

West managed a hollow smile. "Sounds like the man."

As some people came up to the booth to look at the T-shirts, Petey moved to the far side and let the other man handle the sale, and West and Gracie shifted over too. "There was a time when Bo and I were good friends. We had a falling-out and he told me to leave him the hell alone."

West felt that like a punch. There was a real chance here that Petey would know if Bo had had a son.

Petey shook his head. "Generally speaking, most people don't mean it when they say crap like that, but Bo did. I tried a couple times to make amends, but he'd slam the door in my face."

"Sorry," West said. And that explained why Petey had skipped the reception. He'd paid his respects in the way that had felt right to him.

"Are you two married?" Petey directed at Gracie.

She glanced at West, then back at Petey. "No. We're business partners." She seemed to hesitate for a moment, then added, "To be honest, Petey, Bo left my six-month-old son half the Heartland Hollows and I don't know why. We're hoping to confirm our suspicions that Bo had a son named Harry—my baby's father."

Petey stared at them both, then let out a breath.

"Well, I can confirm that. Bo did have a son named Harry."

The punch from seconds ago now felt like a knockout. West laid his hand heavily on the edge of the booth to feel rooted to the earth. Bo had had family.

He'd said he hadn't. But he'd had a son.

And a grandson. Whom he'd known about.

West looked at Gracie and her expression told him what his own must look like. Not quite relief that they'd had it right. Not quite surprise, since nothing in Bo's life the past ten years added up to him having a child out there. And a grandchild.

Except his last will and testament, of course.

Shock was the closest that would describe how West felt right now. In a bad way. The story had to be ugly.

West looked again at Gracie, who was looking at him, too, worry in her eyes. For what they were both about to hear.

Petey shook his head. "I read that the boy—Harry— died in a motorcycle crash. I tried reaching out to Bo about that, but he'd blocked my calls. I'd even tried stopping him to talk when I ran into him in the feedstore a few months ago, but he managed to push past me. And, man, did he look frail."

West recoiled at that. He felt Gracie's soft hand slide briefly into his.

"Sorry," Gracie said to Petey. "Must have been some falling-out," she added compassionately.

"Bo had opened up to me about his son. I didn't know he had a kid."

West felt his eyes widen. *Join the club.*

"But Bo was down that day. He'd been dating someone he actually was thinking of marrying, but she dumped him, said she'd fallen for someone else and was eloping. Man, he was broken up."

West glanced at Gracie and sucked in a breath.

"He was so upset that he uncharacteristically started talking about how he had a child out there he'd never met, never *acknowledged*. A son—twelve years old—in the next town."

West froze. Twelve years old. Like Alexa. He suddenly thought of his daughter in her room, in her purple cave under the window eave, as though she were in Bo's son's position. Wondering why her own father wasn't in her life, didn't want to know her.

He couldn't imagine it. Because such a thing would never have happened.

"I gave Bo some advice about that and he didn't like it. Told me I should mind my own business, and I dug in my heels. I thought we were better friends than that—that my telling him what I really thought would cause such a rift between us. Nothing I said wasn't the God's honest truth. But he told me he wished he'd never said a word about the boy to me. I guess he couldn't handle what I'd said."

What did you say? West almost blurted out. But this felt very personal, and given Petey's conflicted expression, West wanted to be respectful.

"Buy you a corn dog?" West offered, pointing at the booth across the aisle, some open folding tables and chairs beside it.

"Sure," Petey said. "If I tell you what I said to him,

I sure would appreciate hearing that I was right to say it."

West gave the older man a pat on his arm. He had no doubt Petey had been right to say whatever he had. And he was glad Petey would get some peace out of this because he and Gracie sure wouldn't. West had thought he and Bo had been close? *He'd* felt close to Bo. But had *Bo* felt close to West? Had Bo ever shared anything of his life with West? Obviously not.

Unsettled, his stomach tightening, West told himself to just hear out Petey.

Once the three of them were seated, Petey with his corn dog and West and Gracie sharing an order of fries, Petey said, "I'll start at the beginning." He looked up toward the ceiling. "Sorry, Bo, if I'm talking out of turn, but no use keeping secrets when they can help folks. Especially your own kin."

West looked at Gracie. Her expression again seemed to match his own feeling at the moment. *This is gonna be hard to hear.*

Petey chomped on his corn dog, then sipped his cola. "I didn't know much about Bo, but he did tell me some basics. He was originally from a small town a half hour west of here. Raised in foster care. He said his parents and both sets of grandparents died in a bad car pileup on the highway during a bad rainstorm."

West winced. All his family just wiped out. He shook his head. He'd never said a word about growing up in the system.

"We learned recently that Harry's mother was also raised in foster care," Gracie said. "We found that out from her obituary. She died eleven years ago, when Harry was eighteen."

"Ah," Petey said. "However Bo and the lady met, maybe they discovered they had that in common and got to talking."

And more, West thought.

A baby had come from that. And what happened? Why hadn't Bo acknowledged his own son? Met his own flesh and blood?

"Bo always said he wasn't the settling down kind, that he had no interest in getting married. Ladies, sure. But not for the long term. His great love was ranching. Particularly loved raising cattle. Loved horses." He glanced at West. "I guess you know that."

West nodded but had no words.

"The day I ran into Bo at the feedstore—about three, four months ago?—the son showed up."

West and Gracie both sat up and leaned forward, the fries and their sodas ignored. Waiting for Petey to continue.

"This guy, late twenties, just stopped dead in the aisle and said, 'You're Bo Bixby. You're my *father*.' Bo froze up. He turned to look at me, standing there slack-jawed. Bo's eyes were wide, his face white. He then very slowly turned to face the guy."

Gracie glanced at West, tears shimmering in her eyes. She pulled out her phone and showed the man a picture of Harry Ahern. Liam's father. "Was this the guy?"

Petey nodded. "That's him. Hair was shorter, though."

"And they talked?" West asked. "Bo and Harry?"

"First, Harry talked," Petey said. "He was just staring at Bo and finally said, 'I've always known your name and my mom showed me one picture she had of you. I figured you'd come see me if you wanted to. Guess what, you never did.' He then shook his head, looking hurt, disgusted, upset."

West pictured his friend and mentor, in his frail state that time, just a few months ago, confronted with the truth of who he was.

West felt gutted. He looked away, barely able to comprehend what he'd heard.

But Petey was still talking. "Then Harry said, 'I don't even want to know anything. I don't need to anymore. I know who I am.' He started to walk away, but then stomped back over and pointed at Bo and said, 'Actually, I really do. Like father, like son. Because the best person I ever met—Gracie Dawson—told me she was pregnant with my kid and I just walked away like the whole thing never happened. Just like you did with my mother, right?'"

Gracie had gasped at her name.

Petey was quiet for a moment. "Then Harry said, 'I checked the Bear Ridge paper every day for an announcement around the time the baby would be born. And, finally, there it was. June second. A boy. Liam Dawson.' And then Harry stood there and cried."

West and Gracie stared at each other for a moment, both their own eyes misty.

"And then Bo took a step closer to Harry. He said, 'Don't make my mistakes, Harry. Mistakes I've always regretted. I'm sorry. I am. Go see your son.' Well,

Harry got even more upset and just ran off. Bo just stood there. He started rambling a bit to me, but then stopped talking. He looked at me and said, 'You'll keep all this private, right?' I told him I would. Days later, I saw in the Brewer paper that there'd been a motorcycle crash. Harry Ahern was killed." He shook his head then sat with it hung, as if in respect.

West was glad for the reprieve. He needed to just sit there. Not hear another word.

But Petey looked up a moment later. "I tried to call Bo when I heard, but my number was still blocked, apparently. Probably from years ago. I told myself to let it go. I made that promise to Bo that I'd keep it private and I did. Till now. But it felt right to tell you. I think Bo would have come around eventually. But, well..."

But, well...he died.

West's mouth felt stuffed with rags. Between the lump stuck in this throat and the acid churning in his gut, he couldn't even form a thought let alone words.

"Harry never did come see us," Gracie said. "But maybe he'd been considering it. Thinking about it. Maybe he would have too." She burst into tears then.

West turned to her and gathered her into his arms. "I'm so sorry," he whispered.

"I'll give you two some time alone," Petey said, swiping at his own eyes. "I'll be by the booth."

West managed a nod and then held tightly on to Gracie as she cried. His own eyes were stinging with tears but he kept blinking them back.

He hadn't known Bo Bixby at all.

Right there at the end. Three months ago, this had happened. And Bo had never said a word to West.

Hadn't shared it.

"I want to ask Petey something," Gracie said, pulling back and wiping at her eyes. She dabbed at them with a tissue.

West nodded. He threw away their fries and the soda. That neither of them would have any appetite left wasn't even a question.

Hand in hand, they walked back over to the booth, where Petey was sitting again but facing away. He had to be emotional too.

"Mr. Glovers," Gracie said. "I'm wondering about something."

Petey stood. "I'll tell you if I know."

Gracie nodded. "Did Bo ever try to see Harry when he was a kid?"

West was sure the answer would be no. That seemed obvious.

"Well, actually," Petey said, "that was what Bo had been rambling about after Harry had run off. Bo said he *did* go see Harry once, on the first day of school at Brewer Elementary."

West stared at Petey, stunned by this.

"Told me he sat in his pickup and watched at a distance," Petey added. "He said he saw Harry's mother holding hands with a little boy with brown hair who looked just like her. He had a big name tag pinned to his shirt. 'Harry Ahern. K. Ms. Parko's class.' He said seeing that boy scared him senseless, and he drove home. Then he clammed up again and turned and left. I started after him but he waved his hand behind him."

The little boy in the photo. In front of the bushes and chain-link fencing. Beau had taken a shot from his pickup and had it developed.

West was aware that Petey had stopped talking, but he couldn't find his own voice. The lump was lodged back in his throat.

"Petey, thank you for telling us all this," Gracie said. "You've solved a lot of mysteries. Particularly for a baby who'll have questions someday."

West could feel Gracie's eyes on him. He looked at her, then at Petey. "Yes, thank you. Very much."

Petey nodded and swiped at his eyes. "I'm glad you came to see me, that I could get this off my chest and not feel like I wasn't keeping Bo's promise. It was right to tell. It's like an early Christmas present, isn't it?"

For Petey, yes, and he nodded. For himself and Gracie, he wasn't sure. There was a lot to take in.

Bo Bixby and Harry Ahern had both turned their backs on their own children.

Like father, like son...

West felt sick.

He hadn't really known Bo Bixby, the man he'd regarded like a father, at all.

Why is that a surprise, though? You knew he was private. You knew he didn't share.

But that was before West had known just how much Bo had been hiding from him. Hiding from the world.

"Petey," Gracie said. "One thing I think I do know is that Bo laid claim to Harry as his son with a memorial. We found a photo in his house. Of a headstone. That's something. Something big—for Bo." She pulled the photo from her pocket and showed it to him.

Petey looked at it and nodded, his expression heavy. "It might seem like the least he could have done, but it does say something."

West tried to recall that time—three months ago. There'd been a few weeks where Bo had seemed out of sorts, even more reclusive than usual. The timing matched. But he'd been getting frailer and frailer. And West had chalked it up to the illness. A few months after that, he was gone.

West felt tears sting his eyes again and he blinked them back. He wished Bo had opened up. Why hadn't he? How could West have thought they were close when Bo hadn't shared any of this?

"He was ashamed," West said, realizing he was answering his own question. That he hadn't meant to say it aloud.

"Yes," Petey said. "I have no doubt he was. You can try to understand certain people, you can try to wonder about why they did this or that the way you would any ordinary person, but some folks just aren't meant for that kind of examination. They freeze up inside, go cold. They're locked up. It's a terrible way to live, but for them, it actually feels right. Like safety, in a way. I'm no head doctor. But that's what I think."

"I think you're exactly right, Petey," Gracie said. "I'm glad I know the whole story even if it's not the happy ending or at least bittersweet one I'd have hoped for."

West closed his eyes for a second, feeling something

in him, in his chest, tighten. Bo had had this huge secret. A huge, sad secret.

He felt Gracie glancing at him but he just couldn't shake off his gloomy thoughts.

"We appreciate that you shared all this," she said.

He forced himself to focus on the here and now. On Petey Glovers, who he owed for the truth. "Sorry that I'm taking this so hard. Bo meant quite a bit to me."

Petey nodded. "Well, clearly, and vice versa since he left you the place."

Did I? he wondered. *Why would I mean anything to him when his own son hadn't?*

West nodded slowly. He held out his hand to shake, but Petey grabbed it with both his and then did the same with Gracie.

Five minutes later, West barely remembered making his way back to the SUV, Gracie quiet at his side.

"I'll drive if you want to focus on your thoughts," she said.

Practically reading his mind.

"That's a good idea. Thanks."

It wasn't until they were halfway to the ranch that he remembered they were chaperoning the dance tonight. He'd been so looking forward to it. Now, he could barely imagine swaying to music.

But for Gracie's sake, for his daughter's, he'd force himself to put all this out of his mind.

If he could.

Chapter Fourteen

On the drive back to the ranch, Gracie had been able to tell from West's silence and body language that he was deeply unsettled by all they'd learned and that trying to talk to him probably wasn't a good idea. She'd been unsettled, too, but the information had eased something inside her.

Harry had been deeply affected by his father's abandonment. Didn't make it right, of course, to turn around to do the same to his own child. In fact, to Gracie, it made it even worse.

Or just sadder, maybe.

The whole story was just sad.

Maybe that was why she was able to make peace with it. Harry had been troubled. Bo had been troubled. Both of them stuck.

Maybe Harry would have taken Bo's advice and gone to see Liam. Maybe he'd been planning to.

But then fate had intervened.

Gracie decided that was the story. It was the story she wanted to tell Liam when he was older. That she believed in her heart his father was going to come to see him. That his granddad had helped him understand that he should.

But fate. Tragic fate.

She'd gone over this in her head on the drive to the point that she was feeling okay when they pulled up in front of the ranch house.

And since she'd been so preoccupied, she'd let West sit with his own thoughts and just be a hopefully comforting quiet presence beside him. He'd let her know he'd text her what time Alexa would come over so they could get ready together, which had been the plan. Her parents were keeping Liam for the night, so she was all set.

You'll be okay? he'd asked.

She'd nodded and squeezed his hand.

That was two hours ago. She'd gotten a text that Alexa would be by at 5:00 p.m., and he'd pick them up at 5:45 p.m. for the drive over to the middle school. She was glad she'd have little time or bandwidth to think about Harry Ahern and all he'd experienced. Focusing on curling irons, sparkly lip gloss and Alexa's new friend was exactly what she needed tonight.

Besides, the dance would nudge West into relaxing and that was what *he* needed tonight.

You doing okay? she'd texted him an hour ago.

There had been no response for a good twenty minutes. Then, finally, Yeah. See you soon.

Gracie got herself ready before Alexa was due so that she could solely focus on the tween. She had a sleeveless, dark green velvet dress with a V-neck, almost knee-length, which managed to be either casual or dressy depending on how she styled it, so it seemed perfect tonight. Light makeup, hair loose, a gold bracelet, gold and pearl earrings, low-heeled black pumps to keep it more casual, and she was ready to chaperone the Bear Ridge Middle School Holiday Dance.

The doorbell rang, and she knew it would be Alexa solo since she'd walked over.

"Wow, you look so amazing!" Alexa gushed, her eyes wide. She held her purple dress on a hanger over her shoulder.

Gracie smiled. "Thank you!" she said. "I haven't gotten dressed up in a long time. It's fun!" She looked at Alexa's dress. "Your dress is so pretty."

Alexa beamed. "I'm glad I decided not to change the plans." She looked down for a moment, then back at Gracie. "Riley and Lauren don't talk to me anymore. They just ignore me." Her eyes filled with tears. "I mean, I'm really happy I made friends with Alana…"

Gracie took the dress and pulled Alexa into a hug, which the girl wholeheartedly accepted, almost sinking into her. "I'm happy about your new friend too. But it makes total sense for you to feel bad about the other girls. It may hurt for a while."

Alexa let out a sigh and nodded. "Should I put on my dress?" That seemed to brighten her mood.

"Definitely. You change and I'll be back in five minutes."

When she gave a knock on the bathroom door, Alexa opened it in her pretty, dark purple dress, long-sleeved with a scooped neck. It was definitely age appropriate but she could see why West had gotten emotional the other day when Alexa had been transformed with girly hair and a little makeup.

Even with just the dress on at this point, Alexa wasn't the same tween who'd been standing there in jeans and a T-shirt, her long dark hair in a ponytail.

"Before we do my hair, will you help me do my eye shadow again? Everyone's wearing the sparkly sand color. That and the shimmery pink lip gloss."

"Absolutely," Gracie said and got to work, enjoying this very much.

As she used the little brush to sweep on the shadow, Alexa said, "I was telling Jackie that I hope Penn talks to me. Maybe he'll ask me if I want to go get a brownie."

Jackie the cat. Thanks heavens for pets, who made great listeners.

"Maybe he will," Gracie said with a smile.

The girl was radiating with tweenage hope.

Twenty minutes later, curling iron cooling, makeup back in Alexa's small cosmetics bag, the girl was ready for the dance.

Alexa squealed as she looked in the mirror. "I actually like how I look!" She turned left and right, looking behind her shoulder, then face-on. Absolutely beaming. "Thank you, Gracie. You're so awesome!"

"Aww, thank you for saying that. I'm happy to help. Any time."

Alexa was smiling ear to ear. "Do you want to know something?" she asked, suddenly seeming shy.

Gracie looked at Alexa's reflection, but then the girl turned to face her.

"Yes," Gracie said.

Alexa bit her lip. "Sometimes...sometimes I think about what it would be like if my mom was still here. I think it would be like this."

Gracie's heart shifted in her chest. She was so moved, she couldn't speak for a moment. "That's a really lovely thing to say, Alexa. Thank you."

Alexa wrapped her in a hug, and Gracie's heart almost burst. She cared about this girl. Very much. Not long ago, she hadn't even known Alexa and West existed. Now, they'd become so close so fast, their families forever entwined—through Heartland Hollows.

Through Bo Bixby. No matter what West was feeling and processing from all they'd learned today, she hoped he'd remember that. Liam was on his grandfather's land. In his grandfather's house.

West and Gracie had found each other.

And Gracie was standing here with West's daughter, who'd just said something that Gracie would never forget.

Bo had done all this. She would focus on that. Not the past.

And if West was so unsettled by all he'd heard that he'd retreat? That he'd decide they should stick to their original plan, too—and keep their relationship professional.

Something in his expression, in the hard set of his shoulders when she'd dropped him off had left her with that worry.

A little chill ran up her spine at the thought of it getting between her and West. Right now, things couldn't be better. They were in this new phase, where they had decided to take this leap of faith when they'd both been hurt by loss, albeit for different reasons. Trying again was hard. Believing again was hard.

And the story they'd heard was something that affected them both. Bo for West. Harry for Gracie. They were in this together. Surely, West understood that the way she did. They would ease each other through what they'd learned. And could take their time doing so.

Stop worrying, she told herself. *Just take it as it comes. Stop looking ahead. Stop overthinking.*

She and Alexa headed downstairs. They were putting on their coats, since West Calhoun was never late, and, indeed, he pulled up at exactly 5:45 p.m.

Alexa was beaming with excitement about the dance, full of happy chatter about her expectations. Gracie let herself be carried away by it all, her questions shoved to the back of her head.

The bell rang and when she opened the front door and saw West standing there on the porch, two beautiful bouquets of wildflowers, each slightly different, all thought, all worry, went out of her head. She could not wait to be in this man's arms for a slow dance.

This time, West didn't look surprised or uneasy at his daughter's transformation for the event. He looked like a proud father, and Alexa could clearly see it all over his face.

His daughter rushed at him with a hug, the flowers getting smushed.

"You look so beautiful," he told her.

Alexa was beaming even brighter.

"My fellow chaperone does as well," he said, giving Gracie a bow.

Gracie laughed. "You clean up well yourself." He wore a wool overcoat and dark pants and shiny black shoes.

"If you think I'm not getting at least twenty photos..." he said to Alexa with a grin as he pulled out his phone.

Alexa groaned but Gracie could see she was very happy. She posed, even making a few little kid faces in some that Gracie was sure West would treasure.

He was in much better spirits.

Everything is going to be okay, she was relieved to know.

And in a half hour, she'd be in West's arms, where she belonged.

West had worked hard at snapping out of his gloomy mood. He owed that to his daughter. Tonight was about Alexa. She'd been brave to want to go to the dance. And he wasn't going to let anything get in the way of supporting her.

Today had been hard on Gracie, too—full of highly emotional bombshells and revelations—and he was glad that he'd managed to stuff everything down and slam a lid on it. Even if it was just for the next few hours, he could concentrate on being there for Gracie too.

As chaperones, they'd been asked to arrive fifteen minutes early for a brief meeting with the assistant principal on rules and how to handle rowdy behavior.

Alexa had arranged with her friend Alana to show up early as well, so West had left his daughter and her new friend giggling over something by the refreshments table. Lots of small bottled water and platters of cookies and brownies.

There were about ten chaperones, which included a few teachers. The group was standing near where the DJ was setting up, the assistant principal telling them to circulate and just be on the general lookout, that adult presence, particularly friends' parents, tended to deter naughty behavior, so they should sneak in a dance or two or three if so inclined.

West was so inclined. Still.

Despite how heavy the day had been. And despite seeing his daughter all dolled up. Somehow he'd reacted exactly as he was supposed to—like a proud father who'd taken at least twenty photos.

A few of Gracie as well. Serendipitously.

Now, five minutes into the dance, the Bear Ridge Middle School gymnasium was hopping, full of hormonal teens, some dressed up, some dressed down. West glanced around for Alexa and spotted her chatting with Alana near the bleachers, both their hands clasped kind of tightly, and glancing around a bit anxiously as a group of boys on the bleachers seemed of great interest.

Oh, my heart, he thought. *May you have a great time tonight.*

He wondered, very vaguely, which one was Penn.

His little girl's first crush.

He glanced around the room, very aware of Gracie

beside him in that knockout of a green-velvet dress. She looked *stunning*.

Suddenly, she gasped. "Don't look now, but Alexa is dancing with a boy!"

He looked. His daughter was dancing with a boy. With a mop of blond hair that he kept swishing out of his eyes. "This is tough stuff. Watching my baby grow up before my eyes."

Gracie smiled. "I have a feeling that's him—Penn. She'd mentioned his hair."

"It's interesting that they don't move their feet. Just their arms. Is that a Gen Alpha thing? I can't keep the generations between us and theirs straight."

Gracie laughed and wrapped her arm through his. It was probably good thing that just then a song came on that all the kids seemed to love, and a huge rush hit the dance floor so he couldn't see Alexa and the boy anymore.

"Shall we circulate?" he asked, admiring how beautiful she looked.

Her green eyes were twinkling. "Let's."

They walked around, West charmed by the good clean fun. Tonight had been just what he'd needed. To forget the day.

To dance with his lady.

A slow song was now playing, the dance floor clearing quite a bit. Packs of girls were swaying together, some young couples, some chaperone couples.

Including him and Gracie. He held her in his arms, the hint of her perfume driving him wild.

Making him remember the two of them in her bed.

He must have closed his eyes for a second because he felt Gracie's soft lips on his cheek.

"What did I do to deserve that?" he asked, opening his eyes to see her smiling.

"Just felt like it," she said in a sultry whisper. "Somehow, this middle school dance is absolutely magical."

"Right?" he asked, holding her close, looking at her beautiful face. If it were appropriate, he'd give her one hell of a kiss.

The next song was an old eighties' new wave that he'd dance to, but Gracie had taken his hand and was leading him toward the refreshments table. They grabbed two waters and a brownie to split, and dropped down in the folding chairs. Despite being very distracted by his gorgeous date, he and Gracie took their chaperoning duties seriously and kept their gaze on the crowd. So far, he didn't see any bad behavior. No one was grabbing handfuls of cookies and brownies let alone starting fights or tossing around profanities, which were prohibited.

They chaperoned, they danced, they mingled. West had spotted Alexa a few times, another time dancing with that same blond boy, the other times with Alana. She seemed happy, definitely having a good time.

As was he.

Now, close to two and half hours later, the dance was winding down. At least half the kids had left in the past thirty minutes. Dances could be a lot.

"Dad?" he heard Alexa say—clearly upset. "We need to leave *now*."

He whirled around. His daughter looked to be on the verge of tears, her friend Alana nowhere to be seen.

"Alexa, what's wrong?" Gracie asked her.

"Can we just leave, please?" she asked, looking down—and nervously around.

"I'll go tell the assistant principal we need to take off," West said. "Meet you two by the left exit door in a few minutes, okay?"

Alexa nodded and seemed relieved that she'd be able to talk to Gracie alone.

Since the dance was basically over, the assistant principal was fine with him and Gracie leaving, and thanked them for the time, and let him know she hoped they'd be available for the Valentine's Day dance. He said he hoped so.

He could see Gracie and Alexa by the door. They'd already grabbed their coats, so he found his in the long coatracks that had been set up and pulled it on. "Ready?" he asked as he approached them.

Gracie gave him a short smile, which told him things were not good. Something had happened. He looked at his daughter, who again was on the verge of tears. As they left, he could see her friend Alana getting into a car with her parents. If Alana noticed Alexa, there was no wave or smile.

Dammit.

Once they were in the SUV, he waited for someone to fill him in. No one said a word.

"Why did you want to leave early?" he dared to ask.

"Because my one friend hates me now too," Alexa

said, then burst into tears. "You can tell him if you want," she said in broken croaks to Gracie.

Gracie explained, carefully, since Alexa was listening, that Riley and Lauren, Alexa's former friends, had told Alana that Alexa was only friends with her because they'd dumped her. Alana told them that wasn't true, but then the girls asked if Alexa had ever even talked to Alana before she got dumped by them, and Alana realized it was true—that she hadn't. So then she'd confronted Alexa, who'd tried to explain that she just hadn't known Alana before, and it had gone from bad to worse—with Riley and Lauren gloating nearby.

Ugh. It was the kind of middle school nonsense that he couldn't help with because there was no response, no easy *Do this and it'll all be fine*. His daughter had gone from no friends to a new friend back to no friends.

"Alexa, would you like to hear my thoughts?" Gracie said.

Thank God for Gracie. He tried to imagine what he'd say if he were alone with his daughter in the car. Trying to find the right words. He'd screw it up terribly.

"Okay," Alexa said, tears streaming down her face in the back seat.

Gracie turned as fully around as the seat belt would allow so that she could face his daughter. "How about this? What if, when you get home, you call Alana and ask her to hear you out? Even if someone's upset, they usually say okay to that."

Alexa tilted her head. "But what would I *say*?"

"You'll tell her your side," Gracie explained.

Alexa bit her lip. "Which is what, though? I *wasn't*

friends with Alana when I was friends with Riley and Lauren." She gulped in a breath.

Oh, honey, he thought. He could barely remember being twelve, but he knew it was harder on his daughter than it had been on him. He'd had a group of five friends, a few weaving in and out depending on the year. They seemed to have this unspoken understanding that middle school and then high school was hard enough without causing one another problems. So they'd just sort of been there for each other. West was still in touch with most of them, though three had left the state, including Breyer, who he'd been closest to.

"I would have liked to be, though," Alexa added. "She's in two of my classes. She never talked to me, so I thought she didn't want to."

"And if she had talked to you, would you have talked to her back? Like, had a conversation about the class or whatever?"

"Definitely," Alexa said. "I always thought she had the prettiest red hair. Once I even wanted to ask her what styling products she used, but I was afraid to."

"Because you weren't friends? Because she'd never talked to you before?"

"Yeah." Alexa seemed to brighten. "So it's not like I *wouldn't* have wanted to be her friend. I just wasn't sure *she'd* want to. I can tell her that! I even told her about the red hair thing during our study get-together. So she knows I was too shy to say anything before." Her face suddenly fell again. "What if she won't listen?"

"Well, you'll know you tried. And you can try again tomorrow. In person, even. You can go over to her house."

Alexa seemed to be taking all that in. "I could try that. Calling tonight. And see how it goes."

"Sounds like a plan," Gracie said.

"A great plan," West said, but he had a feeling he didn't have a vote here. For a second, he considered asking if that had been Penn, her crush, she'd been dancing with a couple times that he'd seen, but he thought better of it. He'd save that when she wasn't in the middle of a friend crisis.

Alexa had stopped crying and was looking out the window as they approached the turn to the ranch.

Thank you, he mouthed at Gracie. Not for the first time.

She squeezed his hand—and held it.

A half hour later, Gracie was going through the office and making some executive decisions. West had told her she should feel free to turn the room into a home office, since ranch staff never used it as a meeting place—maybe twice in the ten years that West had been at Heartland Hollows.

She thought she might turn it into a family room, though the living room was plenty big. Maybe, for now, she'd just leave it as an office, get used to sitting at the big desk with her laptop. She could turn it into a cozy working space. She'd certainly never had a home office before. Or use for one.

Her phone rang and she grabbed it from the desk. West.

She hoped he was calling with good news about Alexa.

"Hi, thought I'd let you know that I owe you—big. Dinner, a chocolate cake, champagne, box seats to any event you'd like to see. You name it."

She smiled. "I take it that Alexa's call to her friend went well?"

"So well that Alana invited her to sleep over to make friendship bracelets. Apparently, Alana had some friend issues, too, and she got nervous. All is well. And now I have the night free, so if you're up for company, I could bring you the first of many treats as a thank-you. I don't know how I survived parenthood without you, Gracie."

She laughed. "You do just fine on your own. But I'm very happy I was able to help."

"I'll be over in a half hour? We can watch a brainless movie, maybe. It's been such a long, long day that brainless is all I can handle."

"I hear you," she said. "See you in thirty."

In fact, she had a plan to skip the movie entirely and go straight from whatever treats he may bring right into bed.

She'd changed from her dress into a long-sleeved, tunic-style T-shirt and yoga pants and her cat socks, and she was very comfy, so she was ready for West when he'd arrive. She could get his opinion on the office décor. Every time she looked at the three black-and-white and very basic shots of the ranch, horizontal across the wall above the credenza, she felt…nothing. Just fences and empty pastures. She'd like to put up something big and colorful there. Like a saturated shot of a Wyoming landscape. Or even three colorful, fun photos of the cattle at Heartland Hollows. Often she'd look at some of the herd and though they'd just be standing there looking at something, she'd find something precious and interesting and comical in their expression. Or dignified. Yes, she'd replace the kind of serious, dour ones with fun ones.

She brought the desk chair over and hopped up to become instantly taller to remove the photos. And when she took the first one down, there was a kind of small door the photo had been hung against. Hiding. With a very small key in its lock.

Interesting. Given all Bo Bixby had hidden from West on a personal level, she was a little nervous at what she might find behind that little door.

She'd wait for West to come over. They'd open the door together. Maybe *nothing* would be inside, like in his bedside tables, except for the empty box West had mentioned finding, the one that had Bixby written across it. There'd been only one thing in the desk—the photo they now knew had to be Harry Ahern as a five-year-old. She realized that she and West hadn't even had a chance to talk about that. Or anything about Petey Glovers's revelations. Maybe they wouldn't. Maybe they knew what they knew and would leave it be.

Gracie wanted to peek under the two other photos but decided she'd wait for West. Enough surprises for one very long day.

Chapter Fifteen

It was too late to buy any decadent treats from anywhere in town, but West had been sent home with two brownies that had been set aside for each chaperone. They would do just fine. On his way over to the ranch house on foot, he sent Alexa a quick text.

Just checking in with my favorite girl.

She sent back a smiley face emoji, a pizza emoji, and what he thought might be a hot chocolate emoji.

He sent back a heart and pocketed his phone.

West took a deep, cleansing breath of the gorgeous December air, cold but so clean, the scent of Christmas in the air from the evergreens. Next week he and Alexa would go to the Christmas farm in town and get a tree. He'd invite Gracie. He was sure she'd want to bring Liam and choose a tree for the house.

Family. Christmas. Cozy.

He liked the sounds of it. The thought of it.

For the first time today, warm and fuzzy thoughts of his future with Gracie were flattening the unsettling bombshells they'd heard from Petey. He'd taken a breather at the dance, but his focus had been on how hot Gracie had looked in her green-velvet dress. Now, he was thinking about...the future.

He looked up at the stars. A night with Gracie was just what he needed. They'd either make sense of what they'd heard today or let it go—he wasn't sure. He didn't think he'd be up for talking about it. He certainly didn't want to right now. If she did, though, if she needed to go over what they'd learned, if it helped her process, then he'd talk about it.

Because you care very deeply for Gracie Dawson. Somehow she managed to get under that lock and key without you noticing.

That was a lie. He'd noticed.

He laughed at himself and went up the porch steps, shifting the bag of brownies to his left hand and knocking on the door.

The beauty answered and he just wrapped his arms around her, the bag be damned. He needed this hug.

"More of that, please," she said as he let her go only so he could move out of the way of the open door, letting in the cold air.

"I brought our brownies," he said, holding up the bag.

She smiled and took it. "I'll put them in the kitchen for now. I had two cookies at the dance, but I'll never turn down a brownie."

"Same," he said. "Any ideas for our brainless movie?" he asked, and realized he was feeling her out a bit. Seeing if she wanted to veg on the sofa with their treat or talk. He'd be fine with either. Whatever his Gracie needed.

"Actually, there's something I need to show you. I'm a little nervous about what's behind it."

"Uh-oh. Behind what?"

"Did you know there's a locked little door in the office? Behind a framed photograph above the credenza?"

He could feel his face wrinkling in confusion. "Like a safe?"

"I guess. It's not metal. Just a door in the wall. But there's a key right in the little lock."

"Huh. I had no idea. I figured I'd leave any artwork on the walls that were neutral enough."

She led the way into the office. He saw the photo of the landscape on the desk. And when he looked over above the credenza where the photo had been, he could see the little door built into the wall. And the tiny gold key.

"Good lord. Like we need more surprises? What's in there?"

"Maybe nothing," she said. "Like in his bedside tables. And there was just the photo of Harry as a kid in the desk."

"Yeah, but to quote Alexa, that's *a lot*."

She smiled. "I know. There was no way I was gonna open the door on my own. I wanted to wait for you."

"*Do* we want to open it?" he asked. Who said they had to?

"Maybe there's good news in there. Or nothing."

"What would constitute good news?" he asked, staring at the key. "I'm not even sure at this point."

"Me either," she said. "We could ignore it for now. Have some wine and the brownies."

"Perfect suggestion." He was relieved as they left the office and went into the kitchen. He made a pot of decaf while she cut one of the brownies to share.

They brought the coffees and plate of brownies into the living room and sat on the sofa, their hips touching. Even more perfect.

Gracie in kissing distance.

He did tilt his head for a kiss, and she kissed him back, looking right at him with such sweetness, such a feeling of new beginnings. But the moment he was about to take a bite of his brownie, he put the piece back down.

"It's bugging you, too, huh?" she asked, eyebrow raised.

He got up and held out his hand. "I'll be speculating instead of enjoying the movie, enjoying our night. And we need a relaxing night."

She nodded. "Let's see this through to the end, right. We found out today pretty much everything we needed to know about why Bo left my baby half the Heartland Hollows. Now, there's an extra in that wall door. Might as well find out what it is."

She took his hand and stood.

"Maybe it'll be that little something that adds a nice afterglow to a hard story," he said. "We could both use a nice afterglow."

"Oh, yes, we can."

They really could. So they headed back into the office, hand in hand.

They stood in front of the little door built into the wall, both staring at the small gold key.

"You do the honors," he said.

She reached out and turned the key, and the door popped a little. She gave the key a pull and swung open the door.

Inside was an envelope. White, letter-sized. He could see something written on the front.

She scrunched up her face. "I opened it, so you take it out of there," she said.

He sucked in a breath and took hold of the envelope. Not very weighty. He brought it out and held it up so they could read what was written across the front.

Typed: To Liam Hurley Dawson.

Handwritten in black ink: *Bo Bixby*.

Gracie gasped.

West felt his stomach drop an inch.

What the hell was this? What was in there? A letter from Bo to Liam? Grandfather to grandson?

"Is it some kind of explanation?" Gracie asked. "Probably, right?" She bit her lip, eyeing the envelope.

"I would think so," West said. He imagined the letter would say something like, "Dear Liam, I'm sorry I didn't get the chance to meet you. You're my grandson." And so on.

"Should we find out?" He let out a breath. If she said, *Let's open it tomorrow*, that she was exhausted, that they'd both had enough for the day, he'd be just fine with that. After all, it was one thing when whatever might have been in the door was a mystery. Now, it was a letter to Gracie's child.

"I guess I have the right to read it since Bo wanted me to act on Liam's behalf. And whatever it says, it's not like Liam will see it till he's twenty-one. Anyway, I'm sure it will say some necessary things that made Bo feel better—and will make us feel better."

"Agreed," he said with a nod. "Okay. How about if you read it aloud?"

She nodded. "I like the idea of reading it in here. So, if it's something hard to process, we can leave it behind in the office, just sort of close up the room till we're over it. Is that nuts?"

Always on the same page. Love that about her.
Love.

His heart started beating a little too fast. He'd meant that word casually—in that context. But it leapt out in his head now as she stood there, holding that envelope. How he felt about Gracie had always been on the complicated side.

He blinked to bring himself back into the situation at hand. If he was derailed even for a few seconds from an important moment by the word *love*…

"Not nuts at all," he said. "In fact, I think it's necessary."

She sat down on top of the desk. West leaned against the credenza.

"All right. Here goes." She slit open the envelope. There were two typed pages folded in threes. Gracie cleared her throat.

"'Dear Liam,'" she read.

"'One day, you're going to wonder why a total stranger left you half the Heartland Hollows Ranch. Of course, twenty years from now, your mother and West will have long figured things out, not that I made it easy. If they never find the photo of your father's headstone in the gargoyle, well, that's fine with me. I could barely handle seeing it.

I'm a complicated person but, in the end, I am your grandfather. It's hard to type those words since it's not backed up by anything. Except the inheritance and that's something, right? Ranching has always been my life, my lifeline. And Heartland Hollows gave me that feeling of home for the first time in decades. I'm leaving it in two sets of hands. Yours and West Calhoun's.

I could go on—and on. But I've never been a man of many words. I didn't say what I wanted, but in the end, I really didn't know myself. I think that's probably the meaning of life, Liam. The key to happiness. I thought I knew myself but I was wrong.

Yours, Bo Bixby.'"

West had tried to take it all in as he'd listened to Gracie's voice, but he'd get stuck on a word or a line and then felt like he missed something. He was aware that Gracie was reading the letter again to herself. He'd have to do that three or four times to feel like he understood what Bo had been trying to say. Not that Bo seemed to know himself. His point maybe.

His expression must have given that away because Gracie was holding out the letter.

"It's a lot," she said. "I think? But you should read it yourself—and take your time from line to line."

He nodded and took it, then went around the desk and dropped down in Bo's leather desk chair. He read. And read. And a third time.

I didn't say what I wanted, but in the end, I really didn't know myself. I think that's probably the meaning of life, Liam. The key to happiness. I thought I knew myself but I was wrong.

He didn't want to read it a fourth time. Or see it. He folded the letter and put it back in the envelope, setting it on the desk. He looked up at Gracie. "I know what you meant by 'It's a lot' and 'I think?' The only lines that actually explain anything were the last few. About thinking he knew himself but realizing he was wrong."

All the letter had done was dredge up all those unsettling feelings from the conversation with Petey. That West hadn't known Bo Bixby at all. That the man he'd felt so close to, had seen through six months of terminal cancer, had watched take his last breath, had been a stranger.

He hadn't known one thing about the man. One fundamental truth.

That he'd been raised in foster care.

That he'd had a child—and hadn't acknowledged him for five years until something had driven him to go see that child for himself on his first day of school.

He'd taken a photo of Liam, which told West, and he might be wrong about this, that he'd never gone back for a second look. That he'd never tried to see Harry again. Bo had taken the photo and that had been his way to see his son. Or not. What the hell did West know about had been in Bo Bixby's head? His heart. He'd barely had a heart.

Judgmental, he chastised himself. But that was how West felt.

All this had been inside Bo Bixby, particularly in his final weeks when he'd made preparations without West's knowledge. Without West knowing a damn thing about any of it.

You hadn't even considered that he'd leave the ranch to you, so why is any of this so shocking to you?

That was the big question.

And hardly. He shook his head and a pool of bitterness fell into his stomach.

Actually, didn't he know why he hadn't considered it? Because West had always known, deep down, that Bo hadn't felt close to him. Not the way West had felt to Bo. And inheriting half the ranch made him think he'd been wrong. That Bo had felt close to him.

But Bo had kept his entire life, the most fundamental truths, the most painful occurrences—three months before his death—a secret from West.

"West?" Gracie said. Softly at first. And then she called his name again. With concern.

"You're not okay," she said. "So I won't bother with that. Talk to me," she added gently. "How is this making you feel? Because I can't really get a position on how it makes *me* feel. I guess, if I had to put it into words myself, I'd say that in that letter, Bo probably did the best he could."

He gaped at her. "The best he could? *What?* He said nothing of any importance. He didn't offer explanations, let alone apologies." West eyed the letter on the desk, that pool of bitter feelings getting deeper.

I'm a complicated person, but in the end, I am your grandfather. It's hard to type those words since it's not backed up by anything. Except the inheritance and that's something, right?

He shook his head. "Where is the 'I'm sorry I wasn't a father to your father? I'm sorry that my actions—or lack thereof, had such an effect on your dad that he turned out to be just like me.' Where's the 'I told your father that one day we ran into each other at the feedstore that I was sorry, that I was wrong, and he should go see you.' And that Bo believed Harry would have, had the crash not happened." He shook his head again and let out a breath. Exhausted. Spent. He had nothing left in him tonight.

"He didn't say any of that in the letter, but you have the information, West. We both have it. We heard it firsthand from someone who was there."

"We got lucky with that connection to Petey. A chance ask at the feedstore in Brewer led us to him."

"I think Bo figured we'd go on this journey, West. For answers. And we did. We found out everything."

"Everything but—" He stopped, not even sure what he meant. Everything but what? What else did West want to know? Bo himself had said he didn't know himself.

Can't get blood from a stone, his late grandmother used to say. Bo Bixby was a stone.

So why did he feel like such hell here? *Accept it and move on.* West had been through hell on earth when his wife had died, when he'd had to tell his two-year-old daughter her mother wasn't coming home. In language she could understand. Over and over, the language evolving as she'd gotten older.

Why was this letter, this whole thing, hitting him so damned *hard*?

The bitter pool got deeper. His head felt stuffed with cotton.

"Everything but what?" she finally asked, gently. "What do you want to know?" She stepped closer and then sat down in one of the chairs on the other side of the desk. Giving him a little space, he knew.

"I want to know how the person who felt like a father figure to me—for no real reason, apparently, ignored his actual son for almost thirty years—and kept that son a secret. Kept all that happened a secret. I want to know how—and why. But I guess I do know why."

She nodded. "I think I do."

"Like I said to Petey, I think Bo was ashamed. I think that when he was a young man, he decided he was this remote, closed-off man. He had romantic relationships and never committed. He had a son and turned his back. He couldn't handle love in any capacity, West. And he made that okay for himself by deciding that was who he was."

He looked down. It all sounded right. But so? That was it? What was he supposed to do with all this?

Gracie nodded. "Even very close to the end, Bo thought he knew himself. But then he ran into his son. Heard just how his own actions reverberated. How history had repeated itself. And he tried to right it. Remember, West, Bo was frail at that point. When I said he did the best he could in that letter, I mean that. At all the points. Including when he ran into Harry. Including when he wrote the letter. He realized he didn't know himself at all. That knowing yourself is the key to happiness. Think about that. Think about what he was saying there. It *is* a lot."

West closed his eyes. What it *was* was too damned much.

He stood up abruptly. "I didn't know Bo Bixby at all. He was a stranger to me. And he kept it that way until the end. Didn't tell me a thing. Not when his own heart was breaking three months ago."

"He did have a heart and it did break," she said softly. "If we know anything, we know *that*."

West turned away and stared out the window. He could see the big green wreath on the side of the red barn, illuminated by the yard lights. He closed his eyes for a second. He needed air, needed to leave. Needed... what, he didn't know.

"If you want to know what I think, West."

He looked at her.

"I think you were so important to Bo, that you meant so much to him, that he was too ashamed to tell you who he'd been. But he knew you'd find out through the inheritance and the questions. He knew you'd know he *tried* in his way."

He shook his head. "In a million years, I can't imagine ever doing anything like that to someone I care about. Withholding. And then sending them on a scavenger hunt, basically."

"He left you half his ranch. And his grandson the other half. He was trying to make amends. That's what I believe."

Amends. All West knew was that he felt like absolute hell. And that while he'd been in this office, that pool of bitterness had swallowed him whole.

"I need to go, Gracie. And I'm very sorry, but I just need to be on my own. I mean, going forward. For the sake of Heartland Hollows, we should keep our relationship strictly professional. That'll ensure the best outcome for the ranch and for all of us. Because nothing lasts except land. So let's make sure this land is here for Liam and Alexa decades from now."

She'd winced at least three times.

"West, I know you need some time to let this settle. But don't shut me out. Please don't shut me out."

"I can't help it," he said, finally understanding that about Bo. The man hadn't been able to help it. It had taken him over. Just like now. Something had shuttered up around his heart. "I'm sorry, Gracie."

She stared at him, and the pain on her face, in her green eyes, was unbearable. He turned to leave.

She bolted up. "Wait, West," she said. "Just tell me one thing."

He looked at her, hard as it was.

"Do *you* think Harry would have come to see Liam like Bo had told him to?" she asked. "If the motorcycle crash hadn't gotten in the way?"

He looked down. "I don't know."

She winced again. It was clear she didn't like the answer, but it was the truth. He didn't know. How could he?

"I'm sorry, Gracie," he managed on a whisper, everything inside him aching.

Then he did leave, going out the office door through the side yard. Closing the door behind him felt like the goodbye he needed to their romance.

But it just added to how damn bad he felt.

Chapter Sixteen

"Dad?"

West looked up from the kitchen table where Alexa was adding blueberries to the cold cereal in milk he'd served her. She liked to make her own quick breakfasts when she only had twenty minutes to meet the bus, but he'd needed to keep himself occupied every minute this morning.

He hadn't talked to Gracie in two days. There had been no pressing ranch business. No reason to reach out as far as Heartland Hollows had been concerned, and he'd been relieved.

He knew she had to be hurting. And he wished he could take away the heartache, the disappointment. He hated that he'd done that, caused that.

"Earth to Dad," Alexa said.

He snapped out of his thoughts and looked at his daughter. She was staring at him as if he'd grown another nose. "Sorry, honey. I was just thinking about something."

"Gracie?" she asked.

Talk about getting caught off guard. "I, uh..." He stopped. *Get hold of yourself, man. You're talking to your daughter.* "I have lots on my mind." That was true. Probably the truest thing he could say in the moment.

"Like about proposing marriage?" she asked with a grin. "You so are, right? You can tell me, Dad! I saw how you and Gracie were dancing at the dance. At my sleepover with Alana, we were even wondering if you proposed that night. Did you?"

He swallowed. Dammit. "Lex, Gracie and I aren't a couple." *We were, briefly. For a very short, beautiful time.* "We're business partners. Friends," he added so that she wouldn't worry.

Somehow, he and Gracie would become friends again. Time would pass, as it always did. And they'd drift into a basic friendship. That was all he could handle, anyway.

She narrowed her eyes at him. "Friends? Um, Dad, Come on. We saw you *kiss*."

Oh. Dammit again. "Well, we might have gotten caught up in the moment. But when it comes down to it, Lex, Gracie and I need to keep things very professional between us. We're partners on this ranch. You know how people start romances and then break up? Well, Gracie and I can't do that. We have to always be on an even keel to take care of the ranch, make sure it runs smoothly."

Nothing he said was a lie. And he wouldn't lie to his child. But there were some things that he'd keep private.

Now you really sound like Bo, he thought darkly.

"Um, duh, isn't marriage the ultimate partnership?"

Alexa asked, picking up a blueberry and tossing it into her mouth.

He stared at her. "Well. Yes, but—"

"But what? You and Mom would be married if it wasn't for the car accident, right?"

He sucked in a breath, Jenny's face floating into mind.

"And Grandma and Grandpa have been married for almost forty years," she added. "Alana told me her parents even got their vows renewed on their tenth anniversary. They're gonna do that every ten years. Isn't that so romantic?"

He nodded because he couldn't form words. Or a thought. His head was too jumbled. His brain was latching on to some things she'd said.

Proposing marriage.

"I'm just saying that if you and Gracie got married, then she'd be my stepmom." She bit her lip and tears filled her eyes.

He went over to her. "Hey. What's wrong? I told you I'm not proposing to Gracie. We're not even dating, honey. No worries. No one is getting married."

"But I want you and Gracie to get married. I want her to be my stepmom. I really like Gracie. And Liam. He'd be my stepbrother, Dad."

Oh, Alexa. "You like the idea of me getting married?" he asked.

"Well not just to *anyone*. To someone I love too. Gracie."

He almost gasped. "You love her?"

She looked down and bit her lip again, then nodded shyly. "I really do, Dad. She's just so...special."

His heart almost burst. "She is."

"So will you marry her? So she can be my stepmom and Liam can be my stepbrother?" She gasped and looked at the clock on the microwave. "I have to be at the bus in *three* minutes!" She grabbed her backpack.

He grabbed his keys. "I'll drive you down."

With a minute to spare, Alexa was on the school bus. West backed up and then turned around, heading up the long drive. But instead of pulling through the huge open gates with the sign Heartland Hollows, Est. 1899, atop it, he just idled there for a moment. Staring at the name of the ranch.

The place had passed through several ownerships over the years. For this or that reason, it hadn't stayed in the same family.

"Maybe that's one of the reasons you wanted this place in particular, Bo," he said aloud.

"No history."

Except Bo had changed all that in the end, he realized. He'd left the place to Liam. Family. The history would continue. A legacy.

Half the ranch, he reminded himself. Bo should have left the whole ranch to Liam. If he had, maybe West would have found some peace. That Bo had done the right thing, left Heartland Hollows to his *family*.

What Gracie said the other night came to mind. *He left you half his ranch. And his grandson the other half. He was trying to make amends. That's what I believe.*

Because he considered you family, a voice said inside West.

He felt a jolt. Like a lightening bolt of truth.

He left you and his grandson the ranch because you were like family to him. He got out of his pickup and walked up to the gate, looking up at the sign. Heartland Hollows. He pulled off his leather glove and touched a hand to the cold wrought-iron.

I was family. He understood now.

And Bo was trying to make amends in the end. What he'd been saying in the last part of that letter was that he had known himself at the end. That he was able to pass over in peace because he'd finally got it. Family mattered. Harry had mattered to Bo. Liam had mattered.

And West had mattered.

He looked up. "I understand now, Bo."

In trying to make amends, Bo Bixby had brought Gracie and the baby to the ranch—and into West's life.

So thank you, Bo, West said, looking up at the morning sky. The sun was bright, the white clouds floating across the blue. Bo was one of the clouds, West thought. Up there watching and surveying, and aware that the two co-owners were taking good care of Heartland Hollows. That his foreman had fallen in love with his partners—Gracie and Liam.

Yes, *love.*

He smiled up at the sky. He loved Gracie Dawson with everything he had. And he loved that baby boy. His little partner.

For all West knew, Bo Bixby had been doing a little

matchmaking. He knew it wasn't the point of Bo bringing Gracie Dawson to the ranch, but maybe Bo had seen it as a possibility. And seen a continuing legacy for the ranch. For Bo's *family*.

He touched a hand to his heart and once again to the wrought-iron and got back in his truck.

He had somewhere important to be.

Gracie had watched West drive by ten minutes ago, Alexa in the passenger seat. Her heart had clenched hard. How she missed the two of them. For the two days that had passed since West had told her goodbye, she'd been a teary mess. She hadn't told anyone about the breakup. She'd almost broken down with her mom yesterday when Linda and her gram had shown up to take Liam for a few hours. But how could she explain what had happened when she didn't fully understand it herself?

She knew why West was so conflicted. But she wouldn't be able to explain that to her mom and grandmother, and it was so personal that she didn't want to. So she'd just told them she was super busy with ranch business and had a couple meetings with vendors, which was true.

How she'd gotten through those yesterday, she had no idea. But she had.

Now, she stood on the porch, Liam in the baby carrier on her chest. She'd needed some air. And she also wanted to be standing out there when West returned from dropping his daughter at the bus stop. She wanted him to see her and Liam. And to stop and get out and talk to her. Even for a minute.

Gracie wanted to tell him that she understood he needed time. And that she'd be here. If weeks went by and West was still in the same place, well, maybe then she'd reassess and realize she had to emotionally move on. If she could.

But for now, all she knew for sure was that she loved this man. And she was going to tell him so. That way, what had to be said would be said. No hiding anything. No secrets. Everything on the table.

The pickup came into view. He stopped before the drive and she realized he'd spotted her on the porch. He drove around and parked by the house.

And got out.

As she took in the sight of him, this tall, handsome rancher and foreman, she knew that her love for him would be everlasting. She wouldn't get over him. Time would pass, it always did. But she'd never get him out of her heart.

He walked to the bottom porch step. "I realized something just now."

"Oh?"

"When you asked the other night if I thought that Harry would have listened to Bo and gone to see Liam. I said I didn't know. But I do know. The answer is yes. Harry would have gone to see his son. I know that because it's what my heart tells me. And it's what I want to believe."

Oh, West. Same here. She'd thought of that question

a lot the past couple of days. And that was exactly the answer that had come to her.

"It took guts for Harry to march up to Bo in that feedstore. Harry might have seen him around a few times before and been too afraid. But because Harry knew he had his own son, it spurred him on. To confront. To *deal* with it all."

Gracie gasped. "Yes. I hadn't actually thought of that part of it. But, yes. You're absolutely right. And dealing with it would have meant going to see Liam. To change things."

West nodded. He went up the porch steps and stood beside Gracie, facing her.

"I came to quite a few realizations, Gracie. About ebb and flow. That people *can* change. That life can change. You just have to be willing to do it, hard as it may be. Scary as it may be. I think both Bo and Harry were on that precipice."

Tears misted Gracie's eyes. "Yes. Yes, exactly." She brought a hand to Liam's head, covered in the fleece hood over a cap.

"And I realized something else. Something Alexa said."

"Oh?" she asked as he took both her hands in his.

"She told me she hopes we'll get married. Because she loves you and Liam. She wants you to be her stepmother and Liam to be her stepbrother."

Gracie smiled through the tears misting her eyes. "That is so sweet. I love her too."

"So will you make us two the happiest people on

earth? Will you marry me, Gracie? Will you and Liam become our family?"

She wrapped her arms around West as much as she could without smushing her baby boy. "Christmas isn't even for two weeks, but this is some gift, West. Yes, yes, yes. I will marry you. I love you. So much."

"I love you, too, Gracie." He looked at the baby in the carrier on her chest. "We're not just partners, we're family," he said to the little boy.

"Ba la!" Liam said with a big grin, one little tooth poking up from the bottom gum.

They laughed and each kissed him on the cheek. Then they kissed each other, with all the passion and love in their hearts, and went inside to plan a wedding. Right here at Heartland Hollows.

Epilogue

Seven months later...

West's wedding day was picture-postcard perfect. A sunny, breezy, June afternoon with barely a cloud in the sky. Just a few. One of them being Bo Bixby.

West smiled upward as he stood just before the little altar erected in the pasture beside the red barn near the ranch house. A long, red, aisle runner led from the barn to the altar and podium, where a minister would marry him and Gracie.

Husband and wife.

Family.

Everyone special to them was there. Alexa's grandparents, bursting with happiness for not only them, but for their beloved granddaughter. Petey Glovers and his wife were in the third row, Petey with the spirit back in his expression. West had hugged him tight when he saw the man come in with his wife. Bo's lawyer, Garland Jones, was a seated a few chairs down from Petey, dabbing at his eyes already and the ceremony hadn't even started. Several local ranchers and friends he and Gracie had made over the years were all there, sharing their big day.

West's best man, his buddy Breyer, who'd flown in along with a few of West's other friends, waited at the side of the barn. He would walk down the aisle with Gracie's maid of honor, her best friend Miranda, who was right now with Gracie and Alexa in the barn, which had been turned into a bridal room.

He hadn't seen Gracie since last night. Hadn't seen her in her dress.

He couldn't wait.

The Dawsons—well, for now, only Linda and her mom, Dorothea Atwood—were in the first row, across the aisle from Alexa's grandparents. His father-in-law to be was back with the best man, waiting for the ceremony to begin, to walk his daughter down the aisle. Liam, newly one-year-old, sat on his grandmother's lap in his little suit and bow tie, a cowboy hat on his blond hair. For the ceremony, West would hold Liam. Alexa, who was Gracie's bridesmaid, would be beside her.

Alexa's bestie, Alana, was there, as were her parents, with whom West and Gracie had become very friendly. Alex and Alana had become close with two other girls, and now they were happy with their tight group. West had told Alexa she could invite her crush, but it turned out her crush had ended during the dance last winter when he'd done something dumb involving a plate of cookies. Now she had a crush on a different boy. Again with swishable hair.

The "Wedding March" began, and everyone quieted and turned around. The barn door opened and out stepped the maid of honor and the best man, who came down the aisle. Next was Alexa in a pale pink dress. She and Gracie had gone shopping for it together, and Gracie had told her to pick out anything she wanted in the boutique. "Pink, for new beginnings," Alexa had said with a very happy smile.

Gracie had cried when she'd shared that story with West.

And now, the moment West had been waiting for the past seven months, had arrived.

Gracie, his bride, appeared on her father's arm.

West sucked in a breath as she walked down the aisle with her dad. She wore a beautiful, white, lacy gown. Alexa had told him it was called a mermaid-style dress. All he knew was that Gracie looked so beautiful he could barely believe it. She was his. He was hers.

Just when Larry Dawson had taken his seat next to his wife, and Gracie had moved over to face him in front of the podium, Jackie the cat made an appearance. The orange-and-white tabby padded down the runner to the end, where she sat down and began grooming herself, getting a good laugh from the guests. A tiny critter moved in the grass and off she went.

And West, in his tuxedo, held the precious little boy he would raise as his own, love as his own. As he and Gracie said their I Dos, and he kissed his bride, the cheering from Alexa was very loud and happy.

They were married.

West and Gracie had talked about Liam's name, and she liked the idea of changing *both* their names. She'd become Gracie Dawson Calhoun. Liam would become Liam Hurley Dawson Ahern-Bixby Calhoun. When Liam did come of age, if he didn't like that mouthful, well, that would be up to him. But something told Gracie that he would like it just fine.

For now, both she and West loved the richness of the family history in that name.

And, together, the newly formed family of four would create their own legacy.

The End.

* * * * *

Get up to 4 Free Books!

We'll send you 2 free books from each series you try PLUS a free Mystery Gift.

FREE Value Over **$25**

Both the **Harlequin® Special Edition** and **Harlequin® Heartwarming™** series feature compelling novels filled with stories of love and strength where the bonds of friendship, family and community unite.

YES! Please send me 2 FREE novels from the Harlequin Special Edition or Harlequin Heartwarming series and my FREE Gift (gift is worth about $10 retail). After receiving them, if I don't wish to receive any more books, I can return the shipping statement marked "cancel." If I don't cancel, I will receive 6 brand-new Harlequin Special Edition books every month and be billed just $6.39 each in the U.S. or $7.19 each in Canada, or 4 brand-new Harlequin Heartwarming Larger-Print books every month and be billed just $7.19 each in the U.S. or $7.99 each in Canada, a savings of 20% off the cover price. It's quite a bargain! Shipping and handling is just 50¢ per book in the U.S. and $1.25 per book in Canada.* I understand that accepting the 2 free books and gift places me under no obligation to buy anything. I can always return a shipment and cancel at any time by calling the number below. The free books and gift are mine to keep no matter what I decide.

Choose one: ☐ **Harlequin Special Edition** (235/335 BPA G36Y)   ☐ **Harlequin Heartwarming Larger-Print** (161/361 BPA G36Y)   ☐ **Or Try Both!** (235/335 & 161/361 BPA G36Z)

Name (please print)

Address   Apt. #

City   State/Province   Zip/Postal Code

Email: Please check this box ☐ if you would like to receive newsletters and promotional emails from Harlequin Enterprises ULC and its affiliates. You can unsubscribe anytime.

Mail to the **Harlequin Reader Service**:
IN U.S.A.: P.O. Box 1341, Buffalo, NY 14240-8531
IN CANADA: P.O. Box 603, Fort Erie, Ontario L2A 5X3

Want to explore our other series or interested in ebooks? **Visit www.ReaderService.com or call 1-800-873-8635.**

---

*Terms and prices subject to change without notice. Prices do not include sales taxes, which will be charged (if applicable) based on your state or country of residence. Canadian residents will be charged applicable taxes. Offer not valid in Quebec. This offer is limited to one order per household. Books received may not be as shown. Not valid for current subscribers to the Harlequin Special Edition or Harlequin Heartwarming series. All orders subject to approval. Credit or debit balances in a customer's account(s) may be offset by any other outstanding balance owed by or to the customer. Please allow 4 to 6 weeks for delivery. Offer available while quantities last.

Your Privacy—Your information is being collected by Harlequin Enterprises ULC, operating as Harlequin Reader Service. For a complete summary of the information we collect, how we use this information and to whom it is disclosed, please visit our privacy notice located at https://corporate.harlequin.com/privacy-notice. Notice to California Residents – Under California law, you have specific rights to control and access your data. For more information on these rights and how to exercise them, visit https://corporate.harlequin.com/california-privacy. For additional information for residents of other U.S. states that provide their residents with certain rights with respect to personal data, visit https://corporate.harlequin.com/other-state-residents-privacy-rights/.

HSEHW25